Mockingbird in
Mark Twain's Hat

Handwritten inscription:

For Nancy ~
With love from all
the critters in the
Willem Woods ♡
[signature] 2024

Mockingbird in Mark Twain's Hat

KAIA ALEXANDER

ILLUSTRATED BY
ELAINA SCOTT

Waterside Productions

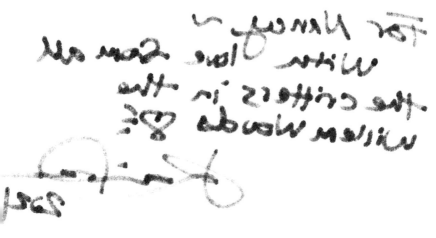

Illustrations by Elaina Scott

Printed in the United States of America

First Printing, 2020

ISBN-13: 978-1-949001-91-4 print edition
ISBN-13: 978-1-949001-92-1 ebook edition

Waterside Productions
2055 Oxford Ave
Cardiff, CA 92007
www.waterside.com

"It is just like man's vanity and impertinence to call an animal dumb because it is dumb to his dull perceptions."
– Mark Twain, from *What is Man?*

TABLE OF CONTENTS

PREFACE

American humorist Mark Twain (1835-1910) was renowned for his novels set in the South. He wrote dialogue the way the words sounded when they were spoken by the characters regardless of spelling and grammar. This had never been done by a writer before. Mark Twain's style revolutionized the way novels were written with his book *The Adventures of Huckleberry Finn* when he gave a voice to the character of Jim, who was a slave. I chose within this narrative to be true to Mark Twain's original style, which illustrated the dialects in this era along the Mississippi River, over a century ago.

I believe that animals and humans have always been friends, and that the dignity of the one is connected to the other. While we all might look different on the outside, we each have a "me" on the inside. We know love, fear, and pain just the same, and I think that under feathers, fur and skin, we're kin. Even a mockingbird can have big dreams, and kindness is appreciated by every animal, large and small.

Each of the characters and all the place names have been borrowed from my own family tree and history going back generations on the Hollan Farm, which was planted by my great grandfather Honey-Pop, and still grows cotton today in Wynne, Arkansas.

Wynne

CH. 1
WYNNE

Somewhere Along the Mississippi River, 1898...

I examined my left wing closely, plucked out one of my straightest quills, smoothed the bark flat before me and wrote:

Wensdy.

I stepped back and admired my word with satisfaction. My penmanship was scarcely more than scrawl, but practice would remedy that. Besides, at only four days old, I dared not let my peck exceed my beak.

My dream was still a secret then, a lofty aspiration tethered to my heart by a photograph of a famous writer by the name of Mark Twain.

Now, I admit I hadn't heard of Mark Twain the day before yesterday, but then a blustery wind intervened. One playful gust ripped several pages of a newspaper from the popcorn vendor's hands at the

Willem County Fair and scattered them, until one torn scrap fluttered down and snagged in the twigs of our nest.

Mark Twain smiled at me from the dusty page. The only words that remained intact from the article were, "Famed Southern novelist and humorist, Mark Twain-" That smile was an invitation with my name on it. I could feel it in my wingtips. I kept the photograph hidden beneath my pocket of the nest so I could pull it out when my family was asleep. In it Mark Twain leaned against a screen door in a wrinkled seersucker suit, smiling mischievously, his face half covered by an impressive grey mustache so furry I thought it looked like a squirrel's tail draped across his upper lip. His hat was bent against the sun.

"Whatcha doin' Wynne?" asked my sister Sissy, peering over my shoulder.

"Nothin'." I turned my back. "Go away."

"If it's nothin' then it ain't nothin' to be secretive about." She tried to see around me but I lifted my wing as a shield.

She tickled my feet and grabbed the photograph.

I snatched it back and tucked it under my wing. "None of your business."

"What's none of her business?" asked my younger brother Possum. He jumped over me and poked his beak in my acorn of blackberry ink, turning his head into a dripping sundae.

I clutched my ink before he could spill any more of it. Sissy took that moment to snatch the slippery bark I was using as parchment and unroll it.

"If you must know, I'm writing a book," I said.

My siblings fell on their backs and laughed, kicking their twiggy legs up in the air, holding their bellies still full of breakfast.

"You hear that, Possum? Wynne says he's writin' a book! You hear that, Earle? A book!"

I felt my cheeks flush, and I turned my back.

My elder brother, Earle, poked his beak in my ear. "Baby brother, you ain't even learned to fly. What makes you think you can write a *book?*"

I peered out over the edge of our nest high in the crepe myrtle tree, pink boa blossoms bobbing in the breeze. "*Haven't.* I haven't learned to fly, Earle, to be grammatically correct."

Earle rolled his black eyes.

This merely spurred me on. "I'm going to be a writer just like Mark Twain," I insisted. "It's my destiny."

"Destiny?" My elder sister giggled with vigor. "Look who thinks he's so smart using grown-up words."

"What's a destiny, Wynne?" whispered Possum.

I put my wing around him. "Destiny means there's something you are meant to do, Possum, and you feel it way down in your bones. When you do it, it makes you happier than anything in the world, and most importantly, it makes the world more wonderful."

"Happier than crickets for supper?"

"Even happier than that."

"Wynne, you're a mockingbird. We only got one destiny, if you wanna call it that, and that's to learn the songs of our woods and sing 'em." Earle lowered his voice, "Don't insult Honey-Pop and our family."

"But Earle," I said. "I can't help it if I want to write a book. We don't get to pick our destiny. It picks us."

CH. 2
JAZZ BIRDS

Fryday.

Singing lessons began promptly at dawn. I was no trumpeter, but my brother Earle made my father proud, prancing across the nest, bellowing the notes that had been heard in our neighborhood since the beginning of the Willem Woods: wren, thrush, warbler, finch, bluebird and cardinal, creaking oak branches, the cicada hum, even the frogs by the stream. We repeated each in succession, three times. But the tunes always got stuck in my throat. What was worse, I just didn't care, and I was terrible at pretending I did.

Honey-Pop, my dad, glared at me in disappointment. "You are shaming this family, Wynne."

"I don't mean to, Pops. I just—I just—"

"I don't want to hear one word. You're a mockingbird and we sing. That's the end of it."

I bowed my head. "Yes, Sir."

Our lesson that particular morning was interrupted by a girl with long auburn braids and a spray of freckles across her cheeks who skipped along the trail beneath our nest on the way to school, singing a pretty melody and whistling the lines she couldn't remember. I tried whistling back, but my father gave me a light smack with his wing and told me never to mock humans.

That evening, on the longest branch of our tree, my mother said to my father, "Give him time." She stroked his feathers and nuzzled his cheek.

Honey-Pop shrugged, exasperated with me. "He's older than Possum, and Possum seems to be taking to the music just fine."

"He's not Possum," she said. "He just needs time."

"He has to learn the songs of our family," he said. "It's in his blood."

"I'll talk to him," said Mama.

Satterday.

Mama began in earnest, "Why don't you give singing a real try? You won't know it's not for you if you don't try."

"It's not my gift, Mama. Earle is the singer. I want to be a writer."

She sighed, then tried to explain. "Wynne, this is how it is. If you ever want a sweetheart, you need to learn to sing."

"A sweetheart? But I don't want a sweetheart."

"Certainly not now, but you will."

"My sweetheart wouldn't love a writer?"

"I don't know, Wynne. Being different is painful sometimes. I think you might grow up to be a lonely bird and that worries me."

"I understand."

"It's my job as your mother to protect you from a fallen future. I want to see you soar."

I nodded, but my plumage drooped, and I sulked the rest of the day.

After dinner, while our parents took a quick flight down to the meadow beyond the creek, I turned to Earle in hopes of a story. "How did Mama and Honey-Pop meet?"

Earle was delighted to recount the tale. Even Sissy bent an ear. Possum, the baby of our nest, hopped over to me and nuzzled against my chest. "Do tell it, Earle," he said. "And don't leave anything out."

Earle cleared his throat. "Our father Honey-Pop comes from a long line of fine mockingbirds, a lineage respected in every wood all the way to the Mississippi River. His father, Tennessee, and his mother, Nonni, raised him here in this very tree."

"Grandpa!" said Possum.

"Yes, indeed. Well, once he fledged he hopped down to the MacMaster's fence each morning in his finest grey suit and regaled the neighborhood with a traditional song that had all the old folks nodding in approval. He pranced back and forth, tail bobbing up and down, eyes closed in the rapture of that sweet jazz, but then he'd open them a crack—just enough to see if the prettiest girl in the Willem Woods would appear. Her name was Hollan. She had the feathers of a fine silk, truly rare bird, hatched from the only egg in her parents' nest, which made her their favorite."

"Mama!" declared Possum.

"Yes, indeed. For three weeks, she evaded Honey-Pop's advances. She was proud and raised to believe she deserved only the best in a bird. Trouble was, she had another suitor by the name of Ricketts, who was once blown in a fierce gale all the way to New Orleans and down to the bayou, where he learned to sing the blues. He had returned from his daring adventure to wed Hollan himself. But if that had happened, we would never have been born."

Possum fluffed his feathers. "But we *were* born!"

"That's right, Possum. But at the time, traditional gentlemen of our woods had no stories to compete with the adventures Ricketts boasted of."

A traditional repertoire for a mockingbird means learning the local jive, the history of your neck of the woods, the way your father sang it. But the blues were taking over, pernicious, creeping like wild kudzu up from the south to overcome the hearts of young mockingbirds who longed to feel a new kind of music in their bones. Our mother was one of these.

"Well, Ricketts had her swooning under the twilight moon, and pretty soon their wedding date was set."

We groaned. It was always the hardest part of the story for us to hear.

"But she didn't marry that ol' goat!" Sissy yelled.

"No sirree," said Earle. "Because rumors spread that Ricketts was spending time down in a gambling parlor on the creek, hiding out with the coons and the skunks and beavers."

"Skunks!" said Sissy, crinkling her nose. "No mockingbird would ever befriend a nasty ol' skunk."

"That's when Ricketts flew off?" I said.

"Honey-Pop chased him into the woods," said Earle.

"Yessir, and he flew away!" said Possum. And it was true. No one in Willem Woods had ever seen or heard of Ricketts again.

"Mama's parents gave her a good talking to about marrying a gentleman and staying clear of vandals, gamblers, and swamp trash that sang the blues. And the next morning she heard Papa's song like it had never reached her ears before."

"And they married and built our nest!" said Sissy.

"True, true," said Earle. "And soon they had four eggs."

"And that was us?" asked Possum.

We all put our wings around him. "Yes, Possum. That was us."

Mondee.

Earle hopped straight up to the top of our crepe myrtle tree. He said he could see the whole world from up there. There was the schoolhouse, the village, the path through Willem Woods, and the boisterous creek that spilled down to the Mississippi River where everyone but the crows were welcome on the banks.

"What else d'ya see?" called Sissy.

"Well," said Earle, turning around. "I see the church steeple. And beyond that there's a whole lotta commotion."

"Come down from there, Earle," said our mother. "It's the Willem County Fair."

"Look Mama," he said, holding up a wing. "I got more flight feathers today. I'm just about ready."

"And me!" said Possum. "I got me some, too!" He held up a scrawny wing with just a few little spikes among all that fluff.

Mama smiled.

I looked down at my own wings, but there wasn't a flight feather in sight. I had plucked them all to use as quills to write my book. It had taken me days to learn to hold the quills just right without breaking one. But I had slowed my own maturity considerably. I clamped my wings to my sides in shame.

That was when my dad swept down to the nest, looking grave. "No one learns to fly this week," he announced.

"But why not?" said Earle. "I got my flight feathers. You promised I was good as ready this week."

"Me too," said Sissy. "You said we could."

"I know what I said, and I take it back."

Mama stopped arranging the twigs in our nest. "Honey-Pop, is this really necessary? You promised the children."

"You promised!" echoed Possum, Earle and Sissy. But not me. I didn't want to learn to fly one bit. I wanted to stay in the nest and write my book. I would have been happy there all my life.

My father opened his beak to speak, but the sky went dark with a flutter of black wings, like a storm coming. A shadow passed over us and we heard raspy caws overhead.

Crows!

We all crouched in the nest.

The sun winked out and the wind rustled in the leaves, and it smelled like rain.

My mother held her breath. "Oh dear," she said. "The little ones are still too young. I thought the crows would be gone another moon."

"What is it, Mama?" asked Sissy.

My mother and father shared a look, deciding whether or not to tell us. Then my mother nodded. "They're going to learn soon enough," she said.

"Crows make supper of mockingbird young," he said.

"But I thought those were just horrible stories!" said Sissy.

"You're all grown up enough now to know the truth," said Honey-Pop. "Because some day it's going to be up to you to protect your own families."

"You don't think they saw the children, do you?" asked Mama.

"No," said my father, "not yet. We'll have to be very careful not to lure them to the nest. Little ones, do your best to keep silent."

We all nodded in agreement and sealed our beaks.

Thirsday.

The crows didn't see us for the first three days after their arrival in Willem Woods. My father sang on the MacMaster's fence while my mother hunted for worms to keep up appearances. The crows did not suspect they were married with a family until the oldest crow hiding in the dead oak saw them both fly into the crepe myrtle tree at the same time. He grew suspicious and alerted the other crows. After that, we almost never slept.

The crows turned their attention to our tree with a savage interest, knowing there were young mockingbirds hidden in the branches. Our parents swept down from the high branches, attacking them and hissing. My father was chased and smacked to the ground more than once before he returned to the nest, bruised and exhausted. My mother tried to distract the crows by guiding them toward the old barn where the spilled corn might make an easier meal.

For one whole week, it was an onslaught. Only one of my parents could rest at a time. The other hissed and chased the crows away from our tree to protect us.

"If I could fly, I could help them," said Earle.

"Now is not the time," Sissy told him. "You have to be an expert to out-maneuver a crow. Look at them turning circles. They're ten times our size."

"And ten times as hungry," said Possum, cringing.

I sighed, my tummy rumbling. "I don't know about that."

Possum had lost weight. So had my sister and I. Since the crows had come, our parents spent more time fending them off than hunting for worms, and we scarcely had enough to eat. We fought over every measly insect presented to us. With the crows always waiting on the offensive, I felt like the woods had eyes watching us all the time. We huddled together and took turns playing "I spy".

That was before we knew we had another, much more dangerous predator to worry about.

The Grey Cat

CH. 3

THE GREY CAT

Fryday.

Possum woke us before the first rays of sunlight struck the church steeple out beyond the woods. "There's something down there in the bushes!" he said, jumping up and down on the nest.

We all sat up and peered over the edge. It was hard to make out anything but shadows in the thin light.

"What did you see, Possum?" asked Mother.

"Raccoon!" he squealed.

"There are no coons in this part of the Willem Woods," said Sissy. "Now go back to sleep."

That was when I saw it, too. "What's that?" I pointed at a tail in the grass.

My father drew a quick breath. Then he hopped up to a higher branch to take a look. That was when the little girl came, fiery braids swinging as she

17

skipped up the trail to the schoolhouse, and the tail disappeared into the brush.

"Probably just a squirrel," said Papa. "No need to worry."

The girl sang a beautiful song about an old fisherman wading in the river, and I wanted to learn that song so I could write it into my story. Her voice was lovely and soothing.

"Wynne, you knock that thought right out of your head," said my dad, seeing what I was thinking. "We do not sing human songs."

"But it's such a catchy tune," I said. "Why not just this once?"

"Because there's nothing more dirty and rotten than humans!" said Sissy.

"Nothing except the Grey Cat," said Earle.

"Earle!" said Mama.

"What's the Grey Cat?" asked Possum, his voice trembling. "Is that what I saw in the bushes?"

"You saw a raccoon," said my father. "A big raccoon is what you saw."

"But you said it was a squirrel," I said.

Just then there was a rustling in the bushes nearby and we all gasped and held our breaths, but it turned out to be a flying squirrel just coming out of the bush and climbing up the Old Oak across the hill. She leaped from one tree to the next, then soared down a few branches to settle on a clutch of acorns. She saw us, gave a little smile, and then nuzzled her mate who appeared from under a mane of leaves.

"You see? A squirrel," said Father.

"What's the Grey Cat?" I whispered to Earle.

"I ain't supposed to say," he said.

"An old nonsense tale," said Mama. "That there was a grizzly old cat in this wood who was blind in one eye, but he was the most terrible hunter of birds that ever lived."

"But what if it's not a nonsense tale?" I asked.

"Of course it is," said Mama. "It's just a tale the old folks of the wood told to keep us in the nest at night."

Father sat us down. "Maybe it is and maybe it's not."

We trumpeted all at once.

"Either way," he went on, "it's why you always have to look before you land. And never go near the porches of humans. They are dangerous places filled with dogs and cats and alligators and other terrible creatures. So long as you stay far, far away from any humans, you will have avoided the greatest of troubles."

My mother sighed. "It's true, but you best add to your list of avoidances all beavers and raccoons, skunks, and foxes, too."

My father whistled and nodded in agreement. "Raccoons and foxes might make a meal of you, but beavers are stupid as the logs they carry, and good for nothin'. We don't associate with skunks neither."

"But why?" I started to ask, but the words knotted in my throat. I knew they wouldn't answer me anyway. Instructions like these were meant to be taken and not questioned.

I took my faded photograph of Mark Twain, rolled it up and slid it under my wing. My dreams were looking far too lofty today, so I thought it best to get some sleep. Maybe I would see new possibilities in the morning.

Sundy.

None of us slept for a week for trembling in fear over the Grey Cat. The crows had left us for now to invade the corn fields, but we were not relieved because in our minds there lurked this new terror. We each took turns watching the dark patches of shadows on the forest floor around the crepe myrtle tree. That was the week Earle learned to fly. He hopped all the way to the top of our tree and swept his wings open and glided right over to the Old Oak.

"Just like a flyin' squirrel!" cheered Sissy.

"Oh boy! You're a real mockingbird now!" said Possum.

I held Mama's wing and cheered for him. Even Honey-Pop cheered. By the end of the day, Earle could turn circles in the sky over our tree, dive to earth and lift off again.

"That boy is a natural," said Honey-Pop.

"He takes after you," said Mama, and snuggled against his feathers.

I lifted one of my wings in the moonlight and looked at the underside where the flight feathers should have been and vowed to stop plucking them.

Mondy.

The crows moved further on down the river, and soon our neighborhood was as peaceful again. Sissy was the next one of us who learned to fly. She hopped up to the edge of the crepe myrtle and opened her wings, letting the breeze pick her up and sweep her toward the Old Oak.

What none of us knew was that three crows had lingered behind, waiting for this day. They swept in out of the sky from nowhere, right down to the tree where my sister had landed.

"Sissy!" we called. "You have to come back to our tree!"

"I can't!" she yelled. "I'm too scared." My sister had frozen there on her branch. The crows alighted next to her.

"Hello, little lady," one of them said. "We see you're out for a morning stretch. Mind if we join you?"

My father flew in like a hornet. He butted the first crow right in the chest, then the second. Mama flew in after him, hissing at the crows to leave my sister alone.

Possum hopped to the edge of the nest, joining in the ruckus. I tugged him back into the nest and told him to keep quiet. Honey-Pop chased the largest crow, and mother tried to help Sissy return to the crepe myrtle. That was when the other crows saw their opportunity.

With both our parents away from the nest, the scruffiest crow landed right in our tree. He was a grizzly old bird, missing feathers all around his beak, but his eyes shone like black buttons. He spread his wings and towered over my brother and I. Earle swept in and gave him a good knock, but with one wing stroke that old crow batted him right down to the ground. Earle got up, shook his head and took off for the sky again.

"I believe I found my lunch," said the Old Crow.

"You might find a much better lunch down in the field over there," I pointed as Possum and I crept backward across our nest, but Possum's foot caught on a twig, and he tumbled backwards off the edge.

"Possum!" I yelled. He bumped and knocked into branches until his foot caught one and he righted himself. The old crow saw his chance immediately and swept in, taking Possum in his beak.

"No!" I yelled, throwing myself over the edge of our nest. I grabbed one of my sharpest writing quills in my claws and jabbed the old crow right in the eye. He dropped my brother as I went tumbling wings over feet toward the ground.

I hardly knew what happened. I had the wind knocked out of me when I hit the ground. When I opened my eyes again the world was blurry and I was moving, fast, an intense heat sweeping across my back, my wings pinned to my body by what seemed to be two enormous white knives.

That was when I heard Sissy yell, "The Grey Cat! The Grey Cat got Wynne! Mama! Mama! Honey-Pop! Save him!"

That meant the wet lump under my belly was the cat's tongue, and all that heat his breath. My wings were pinned between his teeth. I was going to be his supper.

"Wynne!" I heard my dad yell.

"Wynne!" Mama screamed. I called back to them, but there was nothing I could do in the jowls of that great animal. Any thoughts I had were eclipsed by terror, or I would have attempted to free myself. My breath was crushed from my bones, and I closed my eyes, waiting to die.

At the sight of the cat, the crows flew into the sky and disappeared. My father sailed over the cat and drilled his shoulder with his sharp beak. The Grey Cat stopped and sat up, still clutching me in his jaws.

"You do that one more time," he snarled, "and I'll eat him right here."

My father and mother perched on a low branch of a blooming dogwood tree at the edge of Willem Woods, trembling.

"That's better," said the Grey Cat. He took off running.

I didn't hear anyone calling my name now, just my mother, sobbing. I could see the dogwood, the Old Oak and our crepe myrtle tree disappearing out of the corner of my eye, and Possum, his eyes full of tears, watching me. "I'll find you, Wynne! I promise," he said, and I think he yelled something more, but just then the Grey Cat ran through the bushes and came out on the trail, headed for the big red barn at the end of the farmer's field.

I could feel one of my wings about to break, and I tried to be brave. I closed my eyes and wished he would eat me in one big swallow, so I wouldn't have to feel the pain, and that he'd do it far enough away that my parents wouldn't have to see.

It was then, with my eyes closed, holding my breath, that I thought I heard a familiar song. Like angels singing me up to heaven. But it wasn't angels. It was the little girl with the braids.

She screamed and waved her arms.

"You nasty animal!" she yelled. "You drop that beautiful bird this instant!" She took off running after us. The Grey Cat made for the MacMaster's fence, and I knew if he slid through the girl wouldn't be able to climb it, and I would be done for.

The girl ran after us clear down to the fence, where she threw her writing slate at Grey Cat just as he slunk beneath it. I felt the impact as we rolled, and heard the slate break.

Then I was lying on my back in the dirt, and the Grey Cat was darting back to the barn at the end of the field with a patch of fur missing off his rump. He looked back with a hiss at the girl who made a face at him and hissed right back. Then she bent down.

"He's a wicked cat," said the girl, regarding me with enormous eyes full of kindness. "Are you hurt?" She carefully picked me up and cradled me in her warm hands. I was shaking, but I knew I would be all right if I could make it back to my crepe myrtle tree.

Chirp! I said, attempting to explain.

"My, now that's a strong voice, little mockingbird. You must be a brave bird to have survived all that."

She turned me over in her palm and examined my wings. There were spots of blood on my back that she cleaned with the edge of her cotton apron dress.

Chirp! I said again. I was trying to ask her to take me back to the crepe myrtle tree. To my family. But she couldn't understand me.

"Now, I better take you home," she said. "We need to heal up that nasty bite. Then we'll have you flying in no time."

Home. She understood me! My sister and brothers and I would have stories to tell for a hundred years, and I would have the perfect novel out of all of it, complete with a happy ending.

The girl, however, opened the gate and skipped off toward the schoolhouse. She tucked me in a shoebox and shoved it under her desk. By lunch I was so hungry I couldn't keep my mouth shut.

Chirp! I said. *Chirp!*

Soon all the children wanted to see the young mockingbird in the box.

"He's ugly!"

"He hasn't got any color on him except grey!"

"Grey's not a color!"

"I think he's dapper."

"He's got eyes like a rat."

"Maybe he's hungry."

"Where'd ya find him, Mary-Liz?"

The girl smiled. "I saved him from that wicked ol' Grey Cat."

There was cheering, and several of the children went out in the schoolyard during recess with shovels and brought back worms, which I ate gladly. The rest of the day I waited in the dark shoebox to see what would become of me. I cried a little, because I missed my family, but I told myself to be brave and wipe my tears. Besides, I would never have a book without an adventure to write about. This adversity might prove useful.

Tewsday

I woke up in a brass cage inside Mary-Elizabeth's bedroom. I hopped up and down and gave her my loudest chirp.

The door opened and the girl's mother stepped in, a kindly smiling woman who had the smell of dough and other warm-smelling kitchen things about her. "Why, he must be hungry for breakfast. Look at his perfect little grey suit," she said, admiring my plumage. "You did a wonderful thing, you know. Mockingbirds have the most beautiful songs in the world."

She stepped closer to my cage and looked me over. "He's almost fully fledged. He should be fine to eat the worms from the bait shop."

"So I can keep him?" said the girl.

"I don't see why not," said her mother. "At least while he's young. Have you thought of what to name him?"

"Not yet,"

"My name's Wynne," I said. But it came out as a *chirp*, like everything else I had tried to say. The little girl looked at me with her big green eyes in wonder.

My cage was hung in the window so I would have a view across the pasture toward the Willem Woods, where I knew my family was waiting for me.

Escape

CH. 4

EXTRAORDINARY WORDS

Wensdy.

When the little girl went to school the next morning I pulled out my picture of Mark Twain and sat down on the brass swing in the center of my cage to study it. He seemed to be smiling at me, specifically me, as if to convince me that there are no mistakes; that my life was just beginning. But how was I going to get out of the cage and back to the Willem Woods? I pined all day thinking about it. A few times the girl's mother came in and brought me a worm or two, but aside from that, the door was closed and I was left to my thoughts. That was, until the tiny terror of the house appeared.

The smallest of the girl's family was a powerful child of three who seemed to want nothing more than to rip every feather from my body from the first time he laid eyes on me. With a stout frame and hair as yellow as straw, he bowled into his sister's room and spied me in the cage. Within a minute he had a stack of books set on the chair so he could stare into my cage with menacing eyes that spoke of the terrible fate only an overly mischievous child is capable of inflicting on an animal.

He crawled down from his makeshift ladder, only to return with an iron prodder from the family's fireplace. "Stick 'em up!" He shoved the prodder into my cage and I jumped to the swing. "Bam! Bam!" he yelled, poking the instrument at me. "You're dead!"

I leaped and fluttered and shouted for help to avoid certain death at the hands of the little devil. I must have made quite a ruckus because a few moments later the children's mother appeared and yanked him from the stack of books on the chair and ripped the metal prodder from his hands. He wailed and flailed to get it back, but his mother held firm.

"James Edgar, you leave that bird alone this instant!" She crouched down to his level so their eyes met. "If I see you in your sister's room up to no good again, you will not go to the fair with us over the weekend. You can stay here and muck the barn stalls instead. Do I make myself clear?"

The boy twisted his toe into the floor. "Yes, Ma'am."

The boy's mother cupped her hand to her ear. "What's that? I can't hear you."

"Yes, Ma'am!"

"That's better. And this is not a toy. You could poke someone's eye out with this." The boy's mother lifted the iron prod out of reach.

I shuddered in my feathers.

Once he was gone, I made two important decisions. The first was that I had to do everything possible to let my family know I was alive. The second was that I would finish my book. I had learned how to write without breaking my quills, but there was no ink inside my cage and no slippery bark, which meant I had to remember what it was I wanted to say and set it down later.

But there was another, greater problem: I just didn't know as many words as I imagined a real writer would need to write a whole book. What was more, I wasn't too sure how to spell even the ones I did know.

I needed to learn more words, but not just ordinary words; my heart longed for *extraordinary* words. Words that were big enough to describe the sky, and the sadness I felt being away from my family. Words that could make a reader swoon. Yes, I needed extraordinary words.

On these matters, Providence conspired in my behalf. That evening, Mary-Liz pleaded with her father for a new writing slate; she promised to take on twice as many chores around the house if he would. He consented, but under the condition that she not bring home any more wild animals. Her brother's behavior also meant that she could take me with her to school the next day, seeing as that would be the safest place for me till I was fully fledged.

I felt strength rush into my limbs again. Taking me with her to school meant we would pass beneath my crepe myrtle tree, and I could see my family. I nearly turned a flip in my cage when I thought of seeing my parents and siblings again.

But that next morning, Mary-Liz unfolded a faded blue tablecloth and covered my cage. "Wouldn't want that mean old Grey Cat to see you and get any ideas," she said. "I've got to protect you."

At any other moment I might have remembered with gratitude that, in fact, the little girl had saved my life, but this particular morning, I felt crazy inside knowing I would pass right beneath my family's tree we may not even see one another.

The girl unhooked my cage from the beam and pulled it down into her arms. "Now you be brave and don't let anything scare you. It's the last few weeks of school before summer, and I want you to be my show and tell. Maybe you could even sing a song for us." She smiled and lifted the cover and handed me a fat worm. She was such a sweet thing, and I hated to disappoint her with my lack of singing skills. I took the worm and tipped my chin upwards to swallow.

But then it hit me. Singing! If I sang when I passed beneath the tree, my family would hear me.

"Mary-Elizabeth, you're going to be late for school!" The girl's mother called from the front door.

Mary-Liz stepped off the front porch and my covered cage swung back and forth in her hand as I struggled to keep my balance on the little swing. That wicked mischief-maker James-Edgar just stared at us from the front porch; even through the thin cloth I could see the plans behind his eyes.

I felt entirely relieved to be going off to school with Mary-Liz. She began to skip and whistle that tune of hers I loved and always longed to sing. I righted myself on my perch and opened my throat, praying that something useful would come out.

Sure enough, a little song emerged. It wasn't much, but I hoped it was enough for my family to recognize. I continued to sing and sing and sing, chirping and prancing in my cage, hoping to be heard.

I could feel the air cool when we entered the Willem Woods. Leaves crackled under the girl's feet, and the wind became quiet and still. I cleared my throat and belted out the tune. I sang without even taking a breath.

I sang with glory that morning, and confidence. I just knew my family would hear me. Eventually, I paused and waited for their enthusiastic voices. But to my great dismay, there was no response. Not Mama or Papa, not Earle or Possum. Not even Sissy, who had the best ears in the family. I sang and sang, and not a mockingbird in the wood sang back. I never felt so alone, so sad. Then another thought struck me. What if my song wasn't good enough for anyone to know it was me? I hadn't practiced like Sissy and Earle. Maybe I sang like a crow. The even more terrible thought I could hardly bring myself to think: the Grey Cat had devoured them all for supper. I might never see my family again.

There is nothing that silences song quite like losing hope. How was I going to find my family? It fully hit me then that I was a prisoner in the cage, that I might never learn to fly. I hadn't really wanted to at all until that moment, but now that I did, I never would. I held up a wing and checked my flight feathers. They had all come in almost overnight. I stretched out a wing and gave it a little test. I almost lifted myself off the perch—and that was when a big jolt struck the cage, then everything was still.

Quite suddenly, the cloth came off. We were back in the classroom.

"I still say it's an ugly bird," said a little boy, poking his finger through the cage.

"Why, he's grown a lot in just two days," said a little girl with yellow bows in her hair.

"I wanna see if he'll eat this pencil," said a bigger girl with a sneer, and she shoved the pencil into my cage.

"Jenny Larson, you stop that right now," said Mary-Liz. She grabbed my cage and held it in her arms, turning away from the other children.

"Mary-Elizabeth, why don't we keep your fine mockingbird back here until it's time for show and tell?" said the teacher, a tall woman with auburn hair swept into a tight bun.

"Yes, Mrs. Drake."

The morning passed and I learned many useful things. I learned that there is something called the Pacific Ocean, and beyond it a whole continent called Asia. I learned that some people called the Inuit live in the far north where it snows, and they wear sealskin furs and big planks on their feet to keep from falling into the ice. After lunch I learned that great creatures called dinosaurs once roamed the earth, and some of them were so large they would have towered over every tree in the Willem Woods. I sat in rapture. I had no idea the world was so vast.

There was a lunch recess, during which I stayed with Mrs. Drake as she graded papers. Afterward, the class came pouring in again, and Mary-Liz picked up my cage and skipped up to the front of the room, which was a very satisfying place to be since I could see all the faces of the children looking at me.

"This is my mockingbird," said Mary-Liz. "I found him in the woods when that mean ol' Grey Cat tried to eat him. And I saved him and put him in this cage. Are there any questions?"

"What does he eat?"

"Will you keep him?"

"How old is he?"

"Are you sure it's a boy?"

"Can he fly?"

"Wow, he's sure better than a turtle!"

Mary-Liz seemed pleased, and she blushed a little at the attention. I pranced up and down on my perch, lifting my wings and chirping for effect, to show them just what I was.

"He eats worms, and I think he's only a few weeks old. And mother said he's a boy, but I don't know if I can keep him or not. And I haven't seen him fly, but I'm sure he can." Then she curtsied and skipped back to her desk with me. Everyone clapped politely.

I tipped my head and looked at her, this sweet little child who had saved my life. She was certain I could fly? I didn't even know if I could fly, but I tell you—her certainty gave me strength.

The other show-and-tell subjects, in my humble opinion, were not nearly as interesting as I was. They were: a rusted railroad stake, a jar of pennies, a hand-made cricket hutch, a tightly bound ball of colored rubber bands, a violin with a broken string, and a fat and warty old toad.

I spent the rest of the day on the teacher's desk beside the toad, who seemed either stoic or near death. After all my attempts to strike up a conversation failed, I feared he may not survive the afternoon; unfortunately, I was right. Shortly before school ended, he hopped into his water dish and died, which warranted him a splendid funeral in a shoebox out in the yard beneath the chapel gate, attended by all the children.

The following day I was able to forget my worries for the first time.

"Now class, please wipe your slates and we will begin with spelling," said Mrs. Drake. She walked up to the front of the room where she turned to the blackboard with a piece of chalk and wrote nine letters in a row.

I-N-T-E-G-R-I-T-Y

"Can anyone tell me what that word says?"

I had never seen such a fancy word before. I hopped to the edge of the cage, anxious to find out how it was pronounced and what it meant.

"I think I know what it says," said a tall freckled girl, widely considered the brightest girl in the class. "It spells integrate. Like when you merge one thing into another."

"That is very close, Penny. In fact, this word and the word integrate share the same root," said Mrs. Drake.

I tried sounding it out to myself, but I couldn't come up with anything. Mary-Liz twirled one of her braids a few rows in front of me.

That was when I saw it. Right next to the cage. A pot of real ink. I let out a chirp I was so excited, and then clamped my wings over my beak so as not to arouse suspicion.

Beside my cage a ruler was just within reach. With the ruler in my grip I managed to nudge the ink jar right over to the edge of my cage. I tried to reach it and couldn't. Just a little further with the ruler. But my foot slipped and the ink jar wobbled. I held my breath. Two children heard the jar and turned to see me. I pranced back and forth in my cage with my wings outstretched like I was exercising. They looked away.

As soon as they turned around I reached for the glass jar, slowly twisted the metal lid open, dipped in a freshly plucked quill, and wrote my name on a piece of newsprint on the bottom of the cage. I couldn't believe how well the ink wrote, so much better than blackberry ink. This was the real thing.

"I know what it spells," said a small boy in the front row whose hand shot up. His fingernails were dirty, like he had been playing outside. "It spells interfere," he said.

"Not quite, but very close," said Mrs. Drake. "Our word today is 'Integrity'. Please repeat."

The class sat up straight. "Integrity."

"And do you know what it means?"

The little boy shook his head and put his hand down.

"Integrity means soundness of character. Incorruptibility. It means being honest and keeping your word. Having integrity means you treat other people respectably and with fairness. Do you understand?"

All the children nodded, and so did I.

"Now write it down," said Mrs. Drake.

Once I had I copied the word from the blackboard, I held it up and admired it.

Integrity. It was a beautiful word. A truly *extraordinary* word.

In the last three weeks of school with Mary-Liz, I learned one new word each day. There were impressive words like:

R-E-S-P-O-N-S-I-B-I-L-I-T-Y

C-O-O-P-E-R-A-T-I-O-N

And there were smaller words too, words like:

H-A-P-P-Y

L-I-S-T-E-N

A-D-M-I-R-E

There was one word I found delicious, and it was:

L-U-N-C-H

Pretty soon I ran out of newsprint scraps, but that was easily solved once Mary-Liz placed four sheets of brown butcher paper lining the bottom of my cage. I could tear the paper and roll it up and tuck it under my wings, so it was ready whenever I needed to write. Luckily, Mary-Liz always sat me in the same spot on the teacher's desk, where I could see the lesson.

I wanted to be a memorable writer, and I had a suspicion that memorable writers avoided ordinary words, so I set myself to task to learn every word Mrs. Drake wrote on the board. I learned to spell the names of the continents and the oceans, and the states and their capitals. Gradually my spelling improved, and I could write faster.

I even learned to spell the days of the week:
S-U-N-D-A-Y
M-O-N-D-A-Y
T-U-E-S-D-A-Y
W-E-D-N-E-S-D-A-Y
T-H-U-R-S-D-A-Y
F-R-I-D-A-Y
S-A-T-U-R-D-A-Y.

I learned the months of the year and the seasons.

I missed my family so much, and their music was all I had. I found myself whistling my father's tunes in the early morning. And I even picked up a few new songs in school while I wrote.

Our music was jazz, and as far as I knew, the whole idea of jazz was discovering the boundaries of music, then going someplace new. I decided I could start with tradition and then make it *more*. I could sing my father's songs *and* this new music the children sang in class. It didn't have to be one or the other. I had become a both/and bird.

Day after day we passed below the crepe myrtle tree, and every day I sang out to my family, but a response never came. I grew impatient and despairing. Where could they have gone? What had happened? Had the grey cat turned up? Or the crows? I was eaten up with worry. I decided I simply had to escape that dreadful cage and find my family, even if it meant putting an end to all the learning I was doing at Mary-Elizabeth's wonderful school. I had to let them know I was all right, and I wanted to know for certain that they were as well.

Then a sad day came when Mary-Liz didn't take me to school. I woke up early, ready to learn a new word, but instead, she took a ball of yarn from her closet and took to knitting a hat. I sat in my cage in the window all day, waiting to go to school and pass through the Willem Woods, but we didn't go that day. And we didn't go the next day, either. My feathers began to droop. Without new words or a chance to find my family, even worms became uninteresting.

Her little brother came to terrorize me again one evening while his mother was out hanging laundry. This time he was armed with a broom, but I didn't care. He batted my cage like a baseball, back and forth, and I rocked, waiting to fall to my death.

Mary-Liz came in just then and tackled that monster brother of hers. She sent him sailing to the ground, only he cracked his tooth on the edge of the dining table on the way down. This set me to laughing and rolling on my back. The boy screamed for his mother and pointed at his sister, cradling his swollen lip.

When the girl's mother appeared in the door-way she saw the broom and the children and my cage still swinging, and she grabbed her son by the ear and led him out the door. He cried, screaming as if he had been wronged and the world was unfair.

At bedtime the children's mother came in to speak to Mary-Liz, who sat up in bed drawing a picture of me. Her braids were untied, and her face was cleaned of dirt after a day of adventure. Her mother sat down on the bed and began to brush her daughter's pretty hair.

"Now that school is out, I think you should let the mockingbird go. We won't be able to take care of him on the train trip to pick up Grandma and Grandpa on the way to the county fair. What do you say?"

Mary-Liz looked over at me, then dropped her chin. "Do you think Grandpa would take care of him for me?"

"Grandpa is too old to take care of a bird. I think you need to set him free. He looks unhappy in that cage. I think he's ready to fly. What do you say?"

"But I really want to keep him! He's my friend."

"I understand. Well, maybe you can keep him for just a few more days."

"Yes, Ma'am."

"Good girl."

"But will he really learn to fly? I don't want the Grey Cat to get him, Mama."

"Well now, Mary-Elizabeth, he's a grown bird and it's time for him to learn. It's only natural. Look at those feathers on his wings."

Mary-Liz looked forlorn. "I want to take him to the fair. Please, Mama? Please?"

"Time for bed."

I hopped back and forth in my cage and chirped, but no one would answer me. I wanted to go back to the Willem Woods and my family and the crepe myrtle tree.

"See? He likes the idea, Mama."

Her mother smiled. "Good night, Mary-Elizabeth. Lights out, please."

"Yes, Ma'am. Good night, Mama." Mary-Liz leaned up to give her mother a kiss. Then she blew out the candle, turned her head to her pillow and fell fast asleep.

Monday.

The day came for Mary-Liz and her family to catch the train to the county fair. Her mother had agreed, and I would be joining them on the trip. My cage had been cleaned and polished, but it was a large impediment on a train platform. Travelers kept bumping into it, and I was feeling fretful as we heard the first whistle from down the tracks. I had been very careful to make sure all my pages were tucked well up under my wings evenly, so no one would suspect my writing. That little torment, James-Edgar, peered into my cage with a sneer. I could see a plan forming in his eyes, and I admit I was frightened.

The train lurched into position at the station, clanging bells, black and bellowing smoke. The whistle hooted louder than any owl, signaling us to shuffle in and find our seats. The train was already stuffed full of people who had boarded at earlier stops, all eager to reach the fair. We were pushed out to the caboose to ride in the stifling summer heat.

The train snaked along for miles, until every place I'd ever known was reduced to a speck on the horizon; the Willem Woods disappeared, as did the church and the school and the MacMaster's fence. Feeling anxious, I began to flap my wings and chirp. Mary-Liz had fallen asleep on her father's lap, her head tucked under his beard and her legs dangling over my cage.

When we passed through another town and collected more people at the station, the train chugged off, heavy with passengers and all their prize cargo. Fat pigs, freshly groomed mules, squawking chickens, enormous rabbits, and prize watermelons were loaded on the train, and the children screamed, eager to reach the fair.

Soon we were off again, with even more bodies crushed into our caboose. Mary-Liz's mother disappeared to the dining car to fetch everyone some sandwiches. But once she had gone, little James-Edgar—who had been feigning sleep beside his father—snapped his eyes open. With a twisted grin, he lunged at my cage and sprung the door open, and began to grope around trying to catch me. I chirped and fluttered around to avoid his spry sticky fingers.

Mary-Liz and her father startled awake, and she shouted and tried to pull the cage out of her brother's hands. The boy clung tight but stepped backwards and tripped over an old man's cane beside us. With that jolt, both children lost their hold on the cage and the door swung open wide.

Lolly the Beaver

$\mathcal{CH}.$ 5

LOLLY

The children screamed. I watched my world spinning around and around. There was no time to think. I stretched out my wings, and slid through the door just before the cage smashed to the ground. I flapped a few times, and to my astonishment, I just kept going up into the sky. This was no exploratory flight from the myrtle tree over to the oak. I went up and up until the train was as small as a snake in a meadow.

"My mockingbird!" I heard Mary-Liz call out. Her sobs were lost in the roar of the train.

I was free.

Free!

The higher I soared, the more of the world I could see: farmlands, pastures, dirt roads, woods and streams.

This feeling, this exhilarating feeling of turning circles in the sky, pushed along by the breeze, this was a feeling to revel in. For all my grumbling about not wanting to learn to fly, I had taken to it effortlessly and found a splendor I never imagined possible.

I searched for the familiar foliage of the Willem Woods. I circled a few times, rising higher, but I still couldn't see anything familiar. Where was the MacMaster's fence? Where was the little schoolhouse and the broad leaf oaks in the forest? Where were the thick trunk and sinuous branches of our crepe myrtle tree? There was only farmland here, and an occasional swath of meadow, and the creek that wound its way down through the trees. I had no idea how long I had been on that train, but I suppose it had been long enough to carry me far from home. In what direction, I had no idea.

The sun warmed my back as I flew. I knew that if I found the Mississippi River, I could navigate from there toward my home, whether upriver or down. I flew higher and higher to get a good look around, but did not find the river that day or the next.

By night I slept soundly in a willow tree beside the sweet smelling creek, and each day after a quick breakfast, I set out to find my family.

I first approached a woodpecker, but he had no sense in his head for anything except pounding on a hollow tree for grubs. When I asked if he knew the way to the Willem Woods, he replied, "No, sir. No such place I'm 'fraid."

I argued with him for a bit, insisting there *was* such a place, but he found my story difficult to believe. He ignored me once he found a big lazy beetle to pester, and so I flew off to search elsewhere.

No matter how hard I looked, I found only snowy fields of cotton and sprouting corn, patches of shrubs and a few crumbled clusters of rock that jutted from the warming earth.

Breakfast was easy now that I was free from the miserable confines of the cage. I could catch worms and grasshoppers and all kinds of wonderful things to eat. I stuffed myself, content at last. I still missed my family, but I knew they would never want that to keep me from appreciating the goodness in the world around me.

A hummingbird settled beside me that afternoon on a cottonwood tree. I had never seen a hummingbird before. She had an elegant ruby collar, and spoke with an accent I did not recognize, which made her sound like royalty to my ears.

"Hello," I said.

"*Bonjour*," she replied. "It 'tiz a lovely day, iz eet not?"

I nodded in agreement, amazed by how long her beak was, and how tiny her feet. "Where are you from?"

"Eh, you know, I come from zee south, from New Orleans. I should be dere now, except I prefer zee honeysuckle 'ere. Ah, well. *Ne fait rien*."

"Do you know the Willem Woods?"

"*Oui,* I 'ave heard of eet, but never been zere."

"Do you know how to get there from here?"

She tipped her emerald head and fluttered her tiny glass wings. "No idea. *Mais*, I am sure you will find it. *Adieu, cherie!*" Then she darted into the sky and in seconds, she was gone.

The other critters near this creek were even less familiar with the Willem Woods. None had ever voyaged beyond their little homes. I met a grandfather mouse who had lived in his hollow log all his life. He had two-dozen grandchildren climbing on his belly, each competing to kiss his whiskers and curl up beside him in his downy bed.

The young hedgehog I encountered was very kind and wanted to be helpful, but he was recently married and expecting a family. He smiled at me and wished me the best of luck before disappearing into his burrow.

I was losing hope. A week had passed and I had no idea where I was. None of these critters had ever heard of the the Willem Woods. I took to flying higher and higher to get a better look at the surrounding countryside. By night I fell asleep in a cottonwood above the creek with long pleasant branches, good for reclining.

But one night I awoke to the entire tree shaking. First it was just a slight tremor, then a full-out quake. The branches shimmered and swayed and pitched like a ship on a stormy sea.

I woke up irritated and lifted myself into the sky. The moon was still overhead, so I could see the ground illuminated below. That was when I saw the beaver, gnawing away at the tree I had selected as my bed. A beaver! "Hey, what's the big idea?" I said.

The beaver stopped and looked up. "Oh, dear. Oh, oh, dear," she said. "T-t-t-t-t-erribly sorry. I thought this was an unin-unin-uninhabited tree."

I settled on another cottonwood tree above the creek beside the one I had been slumbering in. "It isn't polite to fell a bird's bed in the night," I said, remembering my parent's warning about beavers.

"Terribly sorry," she said. "Won't happen again. My mistake."

"It's all right," I said. "Thank you for the gracious apology."

By then the sun was creeping up and the stars had faded into a cloudy blue expanse of daylight. The lady beaver smiled and yawned, then slunk across the creek to her lodge.

The next evening, having made no further progress in my quest, I was on the edge of the creek hunting for worms when the same lady beaver poked her head out of her lodge to begin another night of felling trees.

"Why, it's you!" she said. "Didn't expect to see you again. You're not from these p-p-p-parts."

"That's right," I said. "I'm from the Willem Woods." She seemed so courteous that I thought just this once speaking to a beaver couldn't be that improper.

"Willem Woods. Willem Woods. Near the river, I ex-ex-expect?"

"You've heard of the Mississippi River?" I exclaimed, fluffing my feathers in delight.

"Met my husband there on the muddy banks. It was a long time ago," she said with a heavy sigh, taking a seat on her haunches.

"You're a widow," I said, realizing what she meant.

"It's been many years now. I came to this safe b-b-b-bog on the river to protect my children, but they grew up and b-b-b-built their own lodges downstream."

"Don't you get awfully lonely?"

"Sometimes. Work keeps my mind occupied. It's not so b-b-b-bad."

"Do you know the way to the river?"

She laughed. "All creeks lead to the river, sure as all rivers lead to the sea. Including this one. Just have to follow it downstream a good ways."

"Why, that's heartening news! I've lost my family and want to find my way home."

"Separation is ruinous, isn't it? I haven't seen my children in at least f-f-f-four summers."

"My name's Wynne. What's yours?" I kicked myself a little to be in such easy conversation with a beaver.

"Folks call me Lolly. Lost one of my teeth when I was trapped years back, so I struggle with my words, f-f-f-forgive me."

"I don't mind. You were trapped? How terrible. You must've made a daring escape."

"Daring? You'd be surprised, young fella, what an ordinary critter will do when it matters most. The men make cloaks and caps of us, you see. My fella and I were caught and caged. But the hunters' boat tipped when it struck a log and my cage fell overboard. Cage door popped open and I swam my way to safety." She sighed and shook her head. "I been on this shore ever since."

"I know how it feels to be locked in a cage. I'm glad you got out."

"It was ages ago. I must be in my last years, you know—I can feel it in my bones. Water's colder than it used to be. I could use one last adventure, though. Say, why don't we search for our family together?"

I thought about it. This was a beaver I was speaking to. My parents had told me never to associate with beavers, skunks and coons. Beavers were, what was it they had said? I couldn't remember. But perhaps not all beavers were the same. Lolly seemed cheerful, and besides, I was lonely. I decided it would probably be all right to be her friend, or at least there was no harm in it for a short time. "Let's do it. When shall we leave?"

Lolly sat down on her tail and preened at her coat. "Sundown."

"Sundown? Oh, dear." I realized then that mockingbirds awaken at dawn, just when beavers are going to bed.

"Not safe to travel by day," she said. "There's hawks near the bend."

I shuddered. I had heard of hawks. Giant birds with beaks that can snap a mockingbird in two, more vicious than any crow. Grown up now I would be no interest to a crow, but a hawk would snatch me from the sky in an instant. "We travel by night then," I swiftly agreed to the graveyard hours.

Lolly smiled. "You're a good-hearted bird, Wynne, I can tell," she said. "Whatcha doin' so far from home?"

"I'm a writer. Well, not a real one exactly, but I plan to be. This whole adventure was an accident."

Lolly chuckled. "I think many adventures must start off by accident. But a writer. There's a talent. I should like to learn some new w-w-w-words. Be a joy to speak with an impressive vocabulary."

"Then I will share with you everything I know," I said with a smile. "An education is useless if it isn't shared among friends."

We set out that evening. Lolly let me perch on her head as she swam in the creek so my feathers could remain dry and we could carry on a conversation. I would whistle a tune to pass the time, and occasionally we would stop for food or to greet a critter on the banks. There were fish and deer, muskrats and toads, but not another of my kind.

I told Lolly of my adventures, of narrowly escaping the jaws of the Grey Cat and of the kindness of Mary-Elizabeth, and the teacher and the children in the school, and how the little girl's brother had nearly been the end of me on more than one occasion. When words fell away, I sang us a jazz melody and reclined, watching the stars wink by.

"How do you expect to find your woods again, Wynne?"

"Not sure, Lolly. I only know the river will guide me. I'll search all my days until I find my family."

"I was thinking, Wynne…"

"'Bout what?"

"The Skumpletun might know how to find your woods."

"The who?" I sat up.

"The Skumpletun is the oldest and wisest of all the animals. You pass through a darkened wood where only owls dare to fly. Beyond the wood is a bog, and somewhere within it lives the Skumpletun. Might n-n-know how to find your family, I bet."

"How do we get there? How soon can we go?" In my excitement I pranced up and down Lolly's spine, tickling her and making her laugh. "Let's find the Skumpletun!"

"Well, I know one someone we can ask. We got to find Rusty."

Creekside Parlor

$\mathcal{CH}$. 6
THE CREEKSIDE PARLOR

L olly waded to shore and I flew up to a nearby birch tree. I thought I could hear a trumpet in the distance and see torchlight up ahead. The vines were thick as night in places, and just as dark. The trees were covered in a veil of ancient moss. As we ambled along in the direction of the light, a cold mist swirled around us and a chill shot through my bones. I began to think this place was not too hospitable.

Up ahead, a shanty house came into view— only this was merely the skeleton of a house. The place had been abandoned long ago and since then had been gradually sinking into the bog beside the creek. The structure had been propped up on stilts to slow its demise. Still, the whole place was a bit crooked, and smelled of stinkweed and dried fish.

The upstairs windows on the house were all boarded, but downstairs there were sparkling lights, and bodies passing by, and laughter.

"There's music!" I said. "Listen."

"You bet there's music. And a whole lot of drinkin' and merry making. It's always like that at the Creekside Parlor. Don't let yourself get drawn in. The characters that come here are mostly weasels. We're lookin' for Rusty. If he's not here, we need to move on downstream."

"Rusty knows where we can find the Skumpletun?"

Lolly nodded. "He'll know."

Lolly stepped up on the porch and the old wood creaked beneath her feet. I fell in behind her. She rapped on the door. A slot opened and a pair of eyes appeared.

"Password."

Lolly cleared her throat. "Buckeye blues."

"Buckeye blues is Tuesday. It's Friday."

Lolly thought it over. "Barnacle stew."

"That was last year," said the grizzly voice behind the door.

"Piggly Miggly?"

"No. Try again."

"I know. It's Lizard G-g-gizzard."

Then one gleaming black eye appeared in the door slot, and the voice that belonged to it had a distinctive air, a kind of put-on accent that could have been from the east. "Forgive my doorman's inhospitable demeanor," said the voice. The door swung open. "Welcome to the Creekside Parlor."

My beak fell open. Standing before me was a mockingbird in a black dinner jacket and a red bow tie, his expression one of pure dignity as he held the door.

Lolly shook herself on the porch, spraying water everywhere, so she could enter the parlor.

The mockingbird made a sour face at this display. "If it isn't Lolly," he said. "We haven't seen you here in ages. Do come in. And who do we have here?"

"This is Wynne," said Lolly. "We come to find Rusty. He here?"

"Oh, he's here. He's always here. Forgive me for being rude. My name is Ricketts." Ricketts stared a hole through my head before extending his wing feathers in greeting.

Ricketts! Could it be the Ricketts of my parent's stories? The Ricketts who had gotten up to no good, hanging out with skunks and gators? I felt myself near about to faint. If this was really Ricketts, I knew I was in bayou country—and in deep. I shuddered and could not bring myself to extend my wing.

"You look like a jazz kind of bird," said Ricketts, eyeing me suspiciously. "But in this parlor, we only sing the blues. Can you dig it?"

Ricketts strode over to a great black piano where a badger was seated and began to sing a mockingbird tune. He had a pleasing, powerful baritone. He strolled up and down in the spotlight and the whole bar stopped to watch him perform. There was a gator in the corner sipping whiskey, a lightning fast squirrel waitress dashing from table to table, and a weasel with a patch on his eye serving drinks at the bar. To my horror, I saw the whole place was full of foxes and skunks and even a few armadillos and coons. A fox looked back over his shoulder at us and drew his hat down over his eyes.

Ricketts went on bellowing the blues until a spotlight caught the wall and a beautiful bluebird on a perch began to sing. She was a truly beautiful singer, and wore a fancy hat dripping with sparkling bottle caps that tinkled as she swung back and forth, raising her elegant wings in emphasis. The whole parlor went wild. A weasel carrying a tip jar conveniently appeared to make the rounds. I was mesmerized by the voice of that blue bird. I had never heard anything like it.

When Ricketts and the blue bird had finished their number, everyone cheered and cheered. Ricketts came over to the bar. "Who's in for a game of cards?"

The coons sauntered over to join the gator and Ricketts at an open table at the rear of the parlor.

"And you!" Ricketts raised his wing toward me. "Be my guest."

I found myself ushered over to the table. "But I don't even know how to play!" I said. "And I don't have any money."

Ricketts thrust a blue chip into my hands. "Why, you've got enough to begin right here."

I struggled to get out of the chair but the two skunks guarding the door twisted their hats on straight and came over. "There a problem?"

I was shaking in my bones. "No. No problem." They had cornered Lolly behind the table. Her eyes confirmed the rising sense within me that something wasn't right.

"Good," smiled Ricketts. "I always wished more of my kind would learn the game." He nodded to the gator, who dealt the cards.

I picked up my hand, and Ricketts stood over my shoulder, indicating what cards I should play. Terrified, I did whatever he said.

Two of the players folded, and that left me and the gator dealer and the last coon.

I lost to the coon, who pocketed my blue chip.

"That's too bad," said Ricketts. "Now you'll have to work off the money you owe."

"But I don't owe any money," I said, confused. "You tricked me! I didn't even want to play this game."

That was all it took. Ricketts nodded to the skunks, who closed in on me. Lolly made a dash to the back and escaped through the delivery door. I followed her, but the weasel blocked the door. "Thief!" shouted the weasel. "He's trying to escape!"

I flew up the stairs to the dark second story of the moldy old house, but all the windows were boarded up. I shoved at the nearest window with all my might. The skunks closed in and one grabbed a fistful of my tail feathers as the rotten board broke and the window snapped open. The skunks lost their hold on me as I was flung outside where I could soar into the trees.

"Lolly!" I called out in the darkness from a high branch. "Are you all right?"

Lolly whistled through her one tooth, and I flew down to the bank of the creek.

"They'll be lookin' for us, now. We best get outta here," she said.

"Why the rush?" said a cool voice in the shadows. We turned to see a fox step out of the darkness, licking his lips, twirling a cane in his paws.

Lolly and I both jumped, but then Lolly smiled. "Rusty! Wynne, this is Rusty, the one we've been lookin' for. He's an old pal."

"Boys back at the parlor shook him up, eh?" said Rusty, his eyes glinting in the starlight. I felt certain it was a look of hunger. "Lolly," I called out, "make a run for it while you still can!"

But Lolly was unperturbed. "We come to f-f-f-find the Skumpletun, Rusty. You're the only one who knows those deep woods. Will you take us?"

"That depends," said the red fox, taking a seat on the bank and curling his fine tail around his paws. "That depends on your story."

I found a bit more courage once I saw the fox had sat down, but I knew foxes were notoriously clever. I flew down from the tree and stood behind Lolly. "I'm looking for my family, back in the Willem Woods," I told him.

"Well, young fella, you got some trouble after you now. Those skunks are just two shakes away, and they'll look for you until Ricketts gets his money. Why should I help a scoundrel like you?"

"Ricketts is a cheater. He forced me into that game so I would lose and have to stay there and work for him."

Rusty threw his head back and laughed. "We all got troubles, kid. Ain't a critter alive without troubles."

I bowed his head. "I just want to go home."

"So if I take you to the Skumpletun, what will that get me?" asked the fox, twirling his cane.

I thought long and hard, but I couldn't think of anything. I looked at Lolly, whose eyes were blank. We had nothing to offer the sly fox.

"Well, I best be on my way," said Rusty.

"Wait!" I called.

But Rusty had already disappeared into the darkness without a sound. Thunder rumbled in the distance, and a soft rain began to fall around us.

"I'm sorry, Wynne," said Lolly.

"You tried, Lolly, and that's more than I could ask for. You're a good friend."

"Well, climb on," said Lolly. "We b-b-best get on down to the river."

And so I climbed up on Lolly's head and we slipped into the creek and around the bend just as the skunks, gators, coons and Ricketts appeared on the creek bed, ready to snatch us up.

"No matter," said Ricketts. "They'll be back."

Constance

CH. 7

CONSTANCE

Lolly and I floated a long way down the creek into the early light of morning. The rain fell harder and harder, like small stones from the sky, and I tried to keep my writing from getting wet by wedging it higher up into my feathers. I had nearly a whole chapter, and I wanted to be certain I kept it safe so that once I finished my book I could find a way to get it published. We traveled the whole next day as well, since the hawks wouldn't give us any trouble in that rain. They'd all flown into the branches for cover.

But by the mid-afternoon the creek was swollen with water, and we were tossed around quite a bit. Lolly pulled herself out on a wide sandbar to rest, and I hopped around in search of caterpillars hiding on the underside of the leaves by the creek.

The heavy rain didn't let up for days. But the worst of it had yet to hit.

Lolly examined our little sandbar and determined that it would be underwater in a matter of hours. "We have to cross to the bank, Wynne."

I swallowed hard. The water was running fast now, and I wondered if Lolly could make it.

"Don't choo worry 'bout me, none. I'll b-b-be just fine. Born for the water, you know." Lolly winked at me.

Soon we had no choice but to cross. The water rose up and swallowed the sand bank, and so Lolly set out nose first at a swift paddle. I flew over her head, urging her on.

Lolly was swept out into the current and pulled downstream as she paddled hard for the opposite bank. Her buoyant brown fur was nearly the same color of the water with all the dirt the storm had dumped into the creek. She was hard to see except for her nose and ears peeking up.

"Come on, Lolly! You're almost there!" I called.

She paddled as hard and fast as her little stubby beaver legs could carry her, but she kept getting swept downstream.

That was when I heard it: a terrible roar from upstream. There was an ominous rumble, like thunder, and it shook the trees. Lightning flashed ahead of us, announcing the wall of water that surged down the creek in its wake. The rapids devoured the banks, the trees, the creek itself. A flash flood!

Oh, no! I pumped my wings and swept up and up to dodge the coming wave, and I called out

"Lolly!" but it was too late. Lolly was swept up in the wall of water like a small twig. She disappeared.

"Lolly!" I yelled again, sweeping the creek looking for my friend. "Lolly!" But who could see anything in that churning mess of water and tree branches, leaves and mud?

The thunder rattled the sky above me, but I kept on in the fierce wind, calling out to Lolly, hoping I wouldn't be struck down by one of the tongues of lightning that flashed all around me. The gale knocked me tail over beak and twisted my wings in a knot that made it hard to fly. I rose and fell, and then lost my balance and began to cartwheel through the canopy.

The next instant, the wind had circled into a rope that hung from the sky, sucking everything from the ground up into its hollow stomach. Before I could fly down to the safety of a nearby tree, I was pulled straight into the heart of the twister, and whipped senseless as I was dragged higher and higher into the sky against my will.

My book was ripped out from under my wings, the pages scattered across the heavens. I could even feel my own feathers being pulled loose, but I held my wings strong and firm. It was the only way. If I crumpled, I would be whipped around like a paper sack.

Up and up I went, straight into the belly of the tornado. All around me were the other unfortunate creatures that had been pulled in as well:

grasshoppers, chipmunks, spiders, ladybugs, and even a hawk. That hawk was no threat to me now. She was just as lost as I was, struggling to right herself, screaming at the wind.

That was when the lightning struck. It flashed down with such force and so close to me that all I saw was white. White sky. White earth. White wind. A lovely glowing light like the moon in the heavens,; it was peaceful here. In the light I could see my family: there was Papa, and Mama, and Earle and Possum, and even Sissy, all smiling at me. We were flying together, wingtip to wingtip, together at last.

That's all I remember.

I woke up and the sun was overhead. It was morning. I was lying on a hard cobblestone, my whole body feeling like I'd been crushed by the hoof of some great animal.

I lifted my head and looked around, then slowly picked myself up and dusted my feathers off. I examined myself for injuries, and everything seemed intact. I spotted the limb of a low hanging oak tree and spread my wings to reach it, but flapped and fluttered like a fledgling. My feet never left the ground.

I lifted my left wing and sure enough, the lightning had singed all the flight feathers to nubs. It was useless. I'd no more be lifting up into the sky than a wheelbarrow could push itself. I looked down and caught my reflection in a puddle: I looked like a rat with wings. Shameful sight to see.

Turned out the tornado had dropped me in the middle of a street. An enormous horse plod towards me, and just in time I hopped out of the way of the giant hooves and cart that followed them. "Whoa," said the driver—just a boy wearing a wide straw hat. He pulled the reins and the old horse came to a walk and then stopped. It snorted and dropped its head, more than content to take a rest.

The boy jumped down out of the cart, and I marveled at his skin, dark as wet clay on the riverbank. His smile was as wide as the Mississippi, white teeth gleaming. He approached the horse and stroked the beast's broad red shoulder. "Whoa, old boy. What'cha got here?" The boy's strong, able fingers glided down the horse's leg all the way to the cannon bone, where he gave a squeeze.

The horse lifted his hoof. The boy examined the underside and clucked his tongue. "Just what I thought." He pulled out a metal pick from his back pocket and scraped at the hoof until a big ol' pebble sprung free and flew through the air in my direction. I leaped to dodge the speeding stone, letting out a *chirp!*

"Well what do we have here?" said the boy, setting down the horse's hoof. He walked over to where I was sitting and squatted down so he could see me better. He tipped the floppy old hat he wore and looked me up and down. "Hello, mockingbird," he said. "Looks like that storm got the better of you. You oughtta' come with me. I'll take care of you." He held out his hand.

I looked at the hand, and then back at his kind smile and twinkling eyes. "Go on," he said, "Hop in. That wing of yours ain't takin' ya nowhere anytime soon. You best come home with us. Ol' Jake here ain't so bad. He's big, but don't let his size fool ya. He's kind as the day is long. Come on, now, I'll catch you some crickets for supper."

At the thought of crickets, my stomach rumbled. And so I decided to be brave, and hopped into the boy's hand. He climbed back up onto the cart and set me on his lap so I could have a place to look out at the world as it went by.

And what a world it was! I had landed in the middle of a gleaming town with brick buildings, slate roofs and wrought iron gates. Spanish moss on the old oaks provided shade in the yards from what was already becoming a fierce summer sun. There were people bustling everywhere to and fro: carts and horses and women in fine dresses twirling parasols and men who walked with their hands up in their suspenders, smoking pipes. It was a fine day, indeed.

Pools of water were drying from the cobblestone streets, and as we rode along the boy smiled and waved at the people he passed.

"Where ya headin' this fine mornin', Robert?" asked a gentleman standing beneath a "United

States Post Office" sign, sweeping out the front walk.

"Good day, Mista Shaw. Down ta the general store. The Mister plum run out of whiskey and we got a steamboat comin' in tonight. Should fill up the whole inn, he says!"

"Why that's fine news indeed, Robert. Fine news indeed. Good day to ya."

"Good day!"

As we rode past the post office, we approached the end of the street where another storefront was just opening. I squinted to make out the sign there that read "New Orleans General Store." Robert reined the horse to a stop.

New Orleans! So, I'd been blown by the tornado all the way south as far as the river flows to the fabled city of ragtime jazz and blues. Robert hopped down from his cart and approached the store owner, a dour faced man who didn't respond to any of Robert's merriment. Robert explained the order and handed the man several coins. The store-owner counted the money three times to make sure it was all there, then pointed around to the back of the building.

Robert led ol' Jake by the bridle around back and began to load the whiskey kegs in the cart.

That was when I heard it. The loveliest sound that had reached my ears since the Willem Woods. It was just a little *chirp!* from a nearby tree. And when I peeked my head over the cart my eyes struck by the most beautiful sight on the great earth.

A mockingbird was hopping across the grass, her ear tipped to the ground in search of insects. She had a slim neck; large, intelligent brown eyes, and a certain shine to her feathers that made her look like an angel from heaven. I sat up and waved hello. She ignored me and went on looking for her breakfast.

"Hello!" I called out, thinking she hadn't heard me.

She looked up, irritated. "Hello to you, whoever you are. You've gone and scared off my breakfast."

"What's your name?" I asked.

She looked up at me with eyes narrowed, then smiled. "Constance."

"Constance," I said. "It's a pleasure to meet you. My name's Wynne."

She eyed the cart I was sitting in.

"Whatcha doin' up there in that man's cart?" she asked.

I hid my singed wing behind my back. "It's a lovely morning and I'm going for a ride!"

But you would think she saw a ghost when Robert came out with the whiskey kegs on his shoulders. Constance took three steps backwards. "Best you find your way home, Wynne." And with that, she flew up into the trees and disappeared.

If only finding my way home were so easy as that. What choice did I have? My life had brought me the way of humans, and so far I'd found some friendly, and some despicable. Why, they weren't much different than our own kind, really. I felt sad seeing Constance go. I wished I could explain everything to her. My heart yearned for a true friend.

When Robert had loaded up the wagon with whiskey barrels, he slapped the reins on ol' Jake's back and we rattled off down the road alongside town that ran along the riverbank. I craned my head to look back at the tall oaks where Constance had disappeared into the leaves, but she was nowhere to be seen.

When I turned around, it was to behold a sparkling sight I'd longed for all the while Lolly and I had been paddling downstream: the Mississippi River!

I chirped and flapped my wings, but did nothing more than succeed in tipping over the hat so that I fell on the seat, landing with the hat on top of me. Robert laughed and righted me, gently picking me up and setting me back into his hat. "So you're excited to see the river," he said. "I bet you've got kinsfolk along the Mississippi, don't cha? I'm sure you're achin' ta see 'em again. The river holds a promise for all of us. You can follow it to freedom. All the freedom in the world is upriver from here."

I looked out on the sparkling water of that wide river and let out a gasp. It was bigger than anything I had imagined. There was so much water! I thought of Lolly, washed down the creek, and I hoped she was all right. She was a beaver, after all, I reminded myself, and beavers are born to swim. But I ached inside just like Robert said, for Lolly, but also for my brothers and my sister, and for my parents. "I promise I'll get home somehow or another," I whispered. "I promise I will."

The old horse clopped on and soon we came to a bend and turned away from the river into another part of town, this time with fancy buildings huddled together down each side of the street. Robert pulled on the reins and we came to a stop in front of a beautiful white building with a sign that read "St. Charles Inn". He threw open the gates and we plodded into the stable yard.

"Robert? Where you been, you lazy boy? You're late!" A man the size of a prize pig in the shadow of the upstairs balcony leaned out and waved a whip.

"Yessir! Sorry sir. I got the whiskey for the steamboat comin' in right 'cher."

"I'll count the kegs for myself." The man's voice rumbled like a storm cloud.

Robert set the hat with me in it on the seat and jumped down then circled around to the back of the wagon where he unlocked the latches on the back and began to unload the large round kegs into the courtyard. His movements were so swift, and he was so strong for a boy his age, you would think those kegs were filled with goose down. He was finished in a matter of minutes, but that was just too slow for the grouchy innkeeper, who came down with his temper on fire.

He grabbed Robert by the ear and said, "You're late, and if it happens one more time you rotten no good son of a slave, I will beat some real sense into you, you got me?" Then he struck the boy across the face.

Robert fell to his knees instantly, hands pressed to his eye, cowering.

"I'm takin' fifteen cents off your pay for bein' late with the whiskey."

"But I wasn't late," whispered Robert.

"You back-talkin' me, boy?" The innkeeper stood over him and sneered, his fat fist raised like a cudgel.

"No, Mista Dixon. I ain't back-talkin', honest."

"Then it's twenty-five cents for bein' late and back talkin', and that bottle of whiskey you drank on the way here."

"But I ain't drunk no—" Robert stopped himself short.

Mr. Dixon reached into the back of the wagon and pulled out a bottle and smashed it on the cobbles. He smiled an evil grin at us before he pushed Robert to his knees in the broken glass and stormed off shouting, "You clean up that mess you made in my courtyard. Any of the horses go lame and you lose your pay for the month!"

Robert swept up the broken glass and then grabbed me and dashed off to his quarters out in the barn. One of the cooks was there waiting. She held out her hand and touched Robert's face and clucked her tongue. Then she got a piece of cold meat from the kitchen and draped it over Robert's eye. "He gonna kill you one of these days, boy."

"I know it."

"Ain't yo fault. You a smart boy, just need a chance at the world. Now, your new friend here looks hungry. Best you both get some supper and then head off."

We were both given plates of hot cornbread and a bowl of beans, and Robert took me to his small room under the stairs that led up to the hayloft.

There, he set me on a three-legged table held up on one corner by a chicken crate. He held me firm but gentle as he lifted my singed wing and clucked his tongue just like the cook had when she inspected Robert's eye. "You're lucky you didn't break it, you know. You must've been caught up in that crazy tornado. I hate to tell ya this, but you're gonna have to stay here awhile until those feathers grow back. I'll catch you a box of crickets tonight that should keep you. Just mind your manners and be quiet if the Mister comes around. He doesn't approve of keepin' wild animals, calls 'em dirty, and he'd beat me blue. Now, we got a steamboat comin' in tonight, so I'll be servin' till late. You get some rest." And he smiled at me with the warmest twinkle in his brown eyes before setting me in a crate and pulling a light tablecloth over the top. He set it near the window for a breeze.

I reached under my wing to pull out my photograph of Mark Twain so I wouldn't feel so lonely, but I forgot I had lost it in the storm. I sat still for a long time in my new prison, feeling sorry for myself. I had never wanted to learn to fly back in the Willem Woods, but now, without the use of my wing, I felt miserable.

But then something happened that lifted my spirits. And it wasn't a something so much as a sound.

From beyond the barn I heard all manner of wonderful singing and clapping in the dining room. All night a host of good-natured folk tumbled into the inn, playin' on the piano like they were born knowing how. Songs of jubilation. Songs of celebration. I closed my eyes and hummed along.

> *Oh, my golden slippers am laid away*
> *Cause I don't 'spect to wear 'em til my wedding day*
> *And my long tailed coat that I love so well*
> *I will wear up in the chariot in the morn.*
> *And my long white robe that I bought last June*
> *I'm goin' to get changed 'cause it fits too soon*
> *And the old grey hoss that I used to drive*
> *I will hitch him to the chariot in the morn.*
> *Oh, dem golden slippers, oh!*

I hummed to myself and then chimed in with the chorus, and felt my spirits lift again. This couldn't be such a terrible place if there was such sweet music in it. My wing would get better eventually. I had to believe I'd see the sky again.

Robert and I woke before the sun the next morning and he took me with him on his rounds to shovel out the stable, sweep the courtyard, and place the morning paper at the doors of each room in the hotel. I had the tune of "Golden Slippers" going around in my head, and perched on Robert's hat I couldn't help myself as a few lines of the melody came out. Robert laughed and sang along.

We reached the last room and as Robert went to toss the paper on the floor, the door swung open and a disheveled old man in a long robe appeared, smoking a cigar. He reached out to take the paper and smiled at Robert. He looked familiar to me for some reason. His hair was strewn about, and the shaggy mustache that hung over his lips parted as he sucked in smoke. But I was whistling away by then, lost in the reverie of my new song.

"Good mornin', Robert. I see you've got a new friend." He narrowed his gaze at me. "Don't I recognize that melody from somewhere, little fella?"

I stopped my prancing and fell silent.

"Now don't get sheepish on account of an old man's morning blather. The mockingbird is God's finest creation, right after the woman. He has a repertoire of over forty sounds and even more calls.

And he's earned my respect as the only bird with his very own alphabet. And you, why you might be the only one of them all who learned to sing a spiritual! Most impressive."

"I found him in Jackson Square yesterday mornin', Sir. Ain't he a fine singer! Just get that wing healed up and he'll be flyin' in no time, I reckon."

But I hardly heard a word that was spoken, because I stood in utter astonishment before my precious photograph brought to life.

Mark Twain.

$\mathscr{CH.}$ 8
WRITING LESSONS

Had I not been so caught up in my song I might have recognized him straight away. This was the honor of all honors! I recovered my manners, bent low and swept my good wing before my breast.

"Why, he's well brought up," declared Mr. Twain. "Perhaps you might bring him by for tea this afternoon, Robert. I could use a little company, and his music is most soothing. I get uneasy when I travel without my wife."

"Yessa," said Robert. "I'll bring him. He might enjoy some company himself."

Mr. Twain tipped Robert a copper, then shut the door to enjoy his morning paper and cigar.

That afternoon, as promised, Robert delivered me to the suite of the one and only Mark Twain. I felt so excited I thought I might jump straight out of my feathers.

When the door swung open, Robert entered the suite and set me on the coffee table. "He'll be good comp'ny for ya, Mista Twain. He's a spirited fella."

"But he won't fly away?" asked Mark Twain.

"Nossa." Robert held out my wounded wing. "Been singed by lightning. He needs some recovery. I reckon that's why Providence sent him to me ta take care of."

"Well, I promise to take care of him in return. Perhaps he'll lend me a little musical inspiration and allow me to read him the latest speech I'm working on."

Robert nodded and left the room, leaving me and my hero alone in the room together.

"You see, mockingbird, the races are next week. The mayor will be presenting the cup in the winner's circle. He's a friend of mine and his daughter is engaged to marry a Yankee, and they want someone respectable to persuade her to the error of her ways. So somehow I've got to manage a speech about horse-racing and proper southern marriage!" He chuckled and pulled out a cigar and lit it. "But what do I know? Love is a madness; if thwarted it develops fast, in my opinion."

I let out a *Chirp*!

"I think you're right, son. I best get to the work of it."

He pulled out a quill and opened a large book on his desk and began to compose his ideas. Soon he snuffed out the cigar and lit another, and rose to pace the room. Oh, how I wished I had my photograph of him to autograph for me! Who would ever believe I had met Mark Twain?

I thought of Lolly, and my family. I thought of Sissy and Earle and Possum. Possum would believe me. Surely, Sissy would. I could see Lolly wink at me and smile. I wanted more than anything to see my loved ones again. Mr. Twain awoke me from my little daydream with a request.

"Do you know any more songs, Mockingbird?" he asked me as he paced.

I knew this was my chance. I hopped over to his desk and picked up the quill, dipped it in ink and wrote one of the words I had learned in Mary-Liz's class.

L-I-S-T-E-N

I straightened my vest and prepared to perform the best rendition of "The Battle Hymn of the Republic" that I could muster, a song I'd overheard many times in Mary-Liz's walks through the Willem Woods.

Mark Twain recognized the melody right away and began to sing along with me. Soon we were carrying on and laughing, and having an uproariously good time of it.

Examining my scrawl on the desk, he remarked, "Tell me, now, this is a very good word, young Mockingbird. Where did you learn to spell?"

I picked up the quill and ink and wrote
S-C-H-O-O-L.

"So you've been to school, eh?"

I nodded.

"Why, that's fine. Very fine indeed. Have you got a name?"

I thought about it, then spelled out

W-Y-N-N-E.

"Wynne. Well, it's a pleasure to make your acquaintance." He reached out a finger and we shook how-do-you-do. "Would you like to learn some new words, Wynne?"

I nodded my immediate interest.

"Good then, I'll be sure to ask Robert to bring you to my suite again this time tomorrow. I'll give you a little vocabulary lesson and then perhaps you can help me finish my speech." He winked.

The following afternoon, just as he promised, Mr. Twain invited me to visit and Robert dropped me off while he completed his chores for the day.

My lesson with him was the most enjoyable hour I'd ever spent in my life—except for those spent in the nest back home in the Willem Woods. I learned the two parts of a sentence: the subject and the predicate. I learned how to spell M-O-L-A-S-S-E-S and M-I-S-S-I-S-S-I-P-P-I. And I learned how a P-E-A-R is a delicious fruit to eat, but you P-A-I-R your socks.

After the first hour had passed, we worked on Mr. Twain's speech together, I on one side of the page and he on the other. We concentrated together for the better half of an hour before Mr. Twain got to his feet and lit a cigar. "Wynne, have you ever considered becoming a writer?"

My heart soared into a billowy contentment at his question. My answer was an emphatic, *Chirp!* Then I began to explain in gesture everything that had happened to me from the day the crows came to the Willem Woods. I wasn't too shabby as a mime, so Mr. Twain picked up everything as I went along.

"You started writing a book. In your box. Nope! Sorry. In your nest. You were nearly eaten by a cat? Then rescued by a, hmm, those must be braids, a girl. But her brother tried to... oh my! Glad you escaped. But you were released.. on a train. How did you get on the train? Then you met a, a, a skunk? No. A fox? Ah, I see the teeth now, a beaver! Indeed. And you traveled down river. Then you came to an old hideaway and got chased by a bunch of scoundrels. Oh, my, that sounds like quite an adventure. Then, what's that? Ah, a storm! Of course. A fearsome tornado. And that was how you singed your wing and ended up here. I see." He sat on the edge of the sofa and puffed on his cigar. "I have an idea, Wynne. What do you say you and I write your story into a book? My publisher has been at me to do something like this, and your story is too good to go untold. What do you say?"

I felt tears come to my eyes, and I shook my head.

"What do you mean, 'No'?"

I raised my wings. Lowered them.

"Ah, I see. There's no ending to your story. You haven't found your family yet. Endings are few and far between, I'd say. Most everything important happens in the middle."

I nodded.

"But Wynne, when you're the author, you can write the ending any way you want it to play out. That's the beauty, you see." He winked at me. "Now we should get to work on this speech. I have only a few days left and it always takes me at least two weeks to come up with my finest improvisations."

So, with that we worked through the afternoon, and then Mr. Twain summoned Robert and requested that he mail a letter for him. "Yessa, right away, Mista Twain." And he slipped the letter down the front of his trousers and invited me to join him on a ride to town. "Mista Twain be needin' his privacy, mockingbird. You and me gonna have a fine afternoon togetha'."

I didn't realize how much I missed the outdoors until I could feel the wind in my feathers while I was perched on the rim of Robert's hat. It was a lovely day with the heat in full bloom as we rounded the crescent of the river and on into town.

Ladies in white dresses promenaded down the streets with parasols in hand. A vendor on the corner was hawking watermelon slices for a copper and Robert stopped so he could purchase one for us. We sat down in the shade of an old tree and ate the watermelon together before we got back in the cart to take the mail down to the post office.

Robert jumped down and went inside with a batch of letters. I could see even from out in the wagon that there was a long line today because of the holiday weekend approaching. I smiled to myself at my cleverness. Why, that made the day Friday. For the first time in my wanderings I knew the day of the week, and I began to feel a sense of hope wash over me. Surely I would find my family again, and we would all be together in the Willem Woods. After all, I had met Mark Twain, the finest writer the world had ever known. I longed to tell them about it.

That was when I saw Constance, perched in the tree just across the street. I whistled to her and gave a wave. "Hey there, Constance!"

She looked back and those beautiful brown eyes of hers, and the graceful curve of her neck just about took my breath away. "Oh, it's you," she said. "Hello."

"Constance, I met Mark Twain! And we're going to give an important speech at the races together."

Just then another mockingbird flew onto the same branch as Constance, and he put his wing around her. "Who's that pigeon down there you're talking to?" he asked her.

"Oh, that's Wynne," she said to this bird, who I now saw was her fella.

I felt my heart sink down into my knobby knees. She already had a suitor, and he was big and handsome and proud. He looked like he could fly circles around the sun.

Before I knew what had come out of my mouth, I jumped the worm and heard myself say, "You know, you could both come to the races as my special guests!"

Constance looked at her big handsome gruff, and he nodded. "That's mighty kind of you. We'll consider it." And he flew off over the church steeple with Constance right behind him. She cast one quick backwards glance in my direction, and then they disappeared.

I was in a downright rotten mood by the time Robert returned from the post office and jumped into the cart. Ol' Jake stamped his irritation at having been left in the hot sun, and snorted as we trotted off.

"What's wrong, Wynne?" asked Robert. "You don't look happy."

I shrugged. My hope had flown off with Constance and disappeared. I lifted my singed wing and pumped the air to test if my flight was returning. I didn't even lift an inch from where I sat.

"Now, now," whispered Robert. "That sky up thar ain't goin' nowhere. It'll be waitin' for you till your wing is good and ready. Take heart. Healin' don't happen overnight."

The next afternoon, Mark Twain invited Robert to stay with us as we worked on his speech. He wanted to have an audience to read to. Pretty soon he had a magnificent speech put together, and I still didn't have the nerve to ask him if I could come along to the races, much less bring guests.

Mr. Twain noticed my mood and commented on it.

"He's been like this ever since that trip ta the post office, Mista Twain. I think he's missin' the sky."

"Come up here, Wynne, and talk to me about it," said Mr. Twain.

I hopped on his desk obediently and perched on his finger.

"You're sure mighty quiet," he said. "Cat got your tongue?" He chuckled at his own joke. Then he held out the quill to me and invited me to spell it out.

I carefully formed the words on the page.
I-N-V-I-T-A-T-I-O-N

"What's he doin' now?" asked Robert.

"He's spellin'," announced Mark Twain.

"You mean to tell me that mockingbird can write?"

Mr. Twain nodded with pride.

"Why, that's remarkable. How's he so learned?"

"You wouldn't believe me if I told you, so I suppose this would be one time the truth would be entirely useless," said Mr. Twain.

"You think I could learn?" asked Robert.

"To write?"

"Yessa. I had this grand idea that I'd like ta be a lawya one day, Mista Twain. Make things fair in the world for colored folk like myself."

"Well, I think the world would be a better place with an honest lawyer in it. Son, I'd be happy to teach you. We'll start with the paper first thing in the morning. You'll learn to read and then to write, that's a promise." Then Mr. Twain looked to me, holding the quill dripping with ink. "Now what's this about an invitation?"

Mockingbird in
Mark Twain's Hat

CH. 9

MOCKINGBIRD IN MARK
TWAIN'S HAT

I found out quickly that Mark Twain never broke a promise. And I remembered back to my days in the schoolhouse with Mary-Liz, when words were written on the board. *Integrity*. What Mark Twain had was integrity. He was a man of honor who kept his word, and I wanted to be just like him.

Robert reported to Mr. Twain's suite first thing every morning to learn to read the paper, and in the afternoons we worked on his speech together until he was satisfied with it. In the remaining time we spent together before supper, Mr. Twain taught me all about what he called "the glamour of grammar." I learned important ideas like "items in a list are always separated by commas" and "a question is always followed by a question mark". It was pure heaven, I tell you, and I cherished every minute.

The day of the races came quickly. I, perched on the brim of Mark Twain's hat, was permitted to accompany him to the racetrack in a carriage sent to fetch him for the occasion.

He was dressed in a fine seersucker suit and wore a pair of polished white loafers that made him look just like the photograph of him I had carried nearly all my life: entirely the gentleman. I felt so proud, sitting on his hat, to be seen with the most famous novelist in the south. I wished my family and Lolly were there to see it!

When we arrived at the track, the people gathered were a picture to behold. Ladies in the most elegant dresses of lace and ribbon with pearls about their necks wandered to and fro beneath colorful silk parasols in the strong sun, shading their faces.

I felt sad that Robert wouldn't be allowed to come with us. Mr. Twain explained that while everyone in town held a fondness for Robert, black men weren't allowed to attend the races. This seemed completely unjust and I chirped my disapproval. "Frankly, I agree, Wynne," said Mr. Twain. "A man is a man, and a good man is not defined by his color or his riches."

I made sure to try and observe everything carefully so I could relay it all to Robert when we returned home. Robert would have loved the races. I felt his absence.

Once inside the grandstand, we were led by a smartly dressed lad in a grey uniform (much like my own feathers) to a box right beside the finish line. The mayor was there with his wife, and a young woman whose cheeks radiated peaches and roses and smelled like soft linen sheets. She had beautiful blue eyes the color of the summer sky. When she spotted me in Mr. Twain's hat she let out a squeal of delight. "Why, a mockingbird! Is he yours, Mr. Twain?"

"'Fraid not. He's just keepin' me company for the time being. Helped me a great deal with my speech, actually." This garnered laughter from everyone in earshot.

I looked around for Constance to see if she'd come, but the racetrack was loud and most dignified birds were frightened off except for a few nosey pigeons pecking at the ground.

The sprightly colts were led out onto the track—brown, white, black and roan—in their flashy bridles and matching saddle pads that displayed their numbers. I watched as the men betted on who would win the race (and only the men, as the women weren't allowed to gamble). The jockeys spit in the dirt and performed their peculiar rituals in hopes of riding to the winner's circle.

Just then another man appeared, young and full of vigor, trotting down the stairs toward the box where we sat. The girl stood up and presented her hand for him to kiss, and she blushed as his lips grazed her glove. But the mayor and his wife looked displeased, and did not even stand to greet the chap.

"Hello, Charlie," they said plainly.

"This must be the Yankee," Mr. Twain whispered. "Bright looking lad. It's a shame they won't give him a chance."

I wondered about this strange new word, Yankee. Was it the same as a foreigner? Why did it make the man someone to disapprove of? This world of men grew stranger every hour I was in it.

"Wynne, kindness is the language the deaf can hear and the blind can see. Anything less is profanity."

As he spoke, the horses lined up in the gate and the crowd fell silent. And then there was a terrible *pop!* of the gun, and the horses ran from the starting line.

They stampeded right by us and the benches shook where we sat. It was one of the most exciting things I'd ever seen. I cheered them on with Mark Twain and the others, whistling my encouragement.

When the horses rounded the final turn, everyone flew to their feet. It would be a close race, with the expected winner trailing the first and second position horses by five lengths.

I cheered and raised my wings in exaltation as the horses sped down the track. I heard another voice cheering behind me, and I turned my head to see who it could be. Of course in doing so, I missed seeing the winner cross the finish line. But I didn't mind in the least, because there behind me was Constance, smiling at me.

I thought for a moment I'd just imagined it. But no. She had come, and what was more, she had come alone even though I'd been foolish enough to invite her and her suitor. I jumped from Mark Twain's hat and bounced across the rail so I could greet her properly, by kissing the tip of her wing feather.

Sadly, we only had that instant. As soon as the winning horse had been wreathed, Mark Twain was on his feet and heading toward the winner's circle with the mayor. He was going to give his speech! I apologized to Constance and jumped from rail to rail and even onto people's shoulders and hats trying to catch him, but I lost him in the crowd. Constance soared up easily and pointed for me. "There he is, Wynne!"

I nodded to her in thanks and slid down the rail all the way to the end, where I flew up into the air and landed squarely in Mark Twain's hat.

"There you are!" he said. "I wondered where you'd gone off to. It's time to deliver our speech. You ready?"

The crowd quieted and the mayor stepped up to the podium. "It is my great honor today to present this silver cup and one hundred dollar prize to the winner of today's race: Huckleberry Suzy! We are so fortunate today to have among us the greatest writer—why, perhaps America's greatest treasure—Mark Twain, and he'd like to say a few words."

The crowd burst into gleeful applause.

Twain cleared his throat and began. His speech was short and sweet, and it drew laughter and cheers from all around, except perhaps from the mayor, who found there wasn't much said of keeping Yankees in their rightful place—namely, away from his daughter. Mr. Twain kept to his usual brevity and wit. When he'd finished, never did you hear such a roar of delight and jubilation from a crowd standing in the hot sun. They smiled and cheered and threw their hats in the air.

That was when I looked around for Constance, and saw her leaving. Her much-too-handsome suitor had come to join her at last, though only to shuttle her away from the festivities. I called out to her, and she looked over her shoulder and smiled at me as she flew away with her fella. I watched her until they disappeared behind the grandstand.

That was my final vision of her, and I knew she was gone. My heart sank. I had the satisfaction of Mark Twain's perfect speech cheering me, and a friendship that I had once only dreamed of. I had to let that be enough.

Back at the inn, Robert greeted us enthusiastically.

"Big day for a little bird," said Mark Twain. "He thrilled the crowd, Robert. I'm sure he'll tell you all about the races."

Mr. Twain picked me up in his hands so he could look me in the eye. "Surely that wing has healed up by now, you think?"

I shook my head.

He leaned in close and examined my wing with his spectacles. "Robert, take a look there. Wynne is growing his feathers back!"

This surprised me as much as it did Robert. I examined my wing and sure enough, there were dozens of new feathers growing in firm and strong. I beat the air to feel if it could support my weight. Not yet. Almost.

"Now, Wynne, I've got some news for you," said Mr. Twain. "I'm only here for one more week, and then I'm headed upriver to meet my wife so we can travel together to our home in Connecticut. I'd like to invite you to come along. Both of you. What do you say?" Turning to Robert, he added, "I'll pay your fare and we'll head upriver to where there's more opportunity for the aspirations of a literate young man." Mr. Twain smiled at Robert.

Robert shook his head. "The Mista here won't let me. It's no use. I owe him money for my board, and every time I work hard enough to stop owin', he start subtractin' money from my pay so I'll always owe him. Makin' up stories like I drank a bottle o' whiskey or I spoiled the milk. Don't matter. Always the same. He'll never let me stop owin'."

I thought about Ricketts and his trick back at the Creekside Parlor. I would have been stuck in Robert's position myself if I hadn't escaped.

I picked up my quill, quickly scrawled a word and held the page for Mark Twain to read. "Ah, I see. Yes, that's right, mockingbird. Mr. Dixon is an unkind man."

Robert sighed. "Yessiree."

Mark Twain shook his head and closed his eyes. "You just leave Mr. Dixon to me, Robert."

The Skumpleton

CH. 10

THE SKUMPLETON

Sure enough, I watched through the dirty window the next day as Mark Twain paid Robert's falsified debts in the accounting office, and Mr. Dixon seemed downright happy to snap his suspenders and close his fat fingers around the coins in his palm.

As we reached the road, Robert let out a shriek of pure jubilation and threw his hat into the air. "I'm free, Mista Twain! And I owe it all to you, sir."

"Make me the promise that you will never miss a day of your education."

"I promise, sir," said Robert, holding his hat. "I will be in school every day until the day I'm a lawyer, you can count on that."

Saying goodbye to New Orleans wasn't so difficult for me. I put my mind on my writing, and the river before me. All my other adventures were behind me now. I had a fresh page, a blank slate, and I welcomed it.

Mark Twain smiled, satisfied.

The ferryboat was an extraordinary creature that lumbered along, rumbling a constant tune. Twain, having once been a riverboat pilot, found his way to the captain's side and watched the familiar stretches of his favorite river come into view. He spent hours up there, reading the water, complimenting the pilot, and soaking in what he knew might be his last trip up his beloved Mississippi.

Robert had never been on a riverboat before. He never stopped grinning, so eager was he to reach that new life of his dreams. He wanted to get his degree and set up a law practice, then find himself a wife. He also planned to look for his father, who had disappeared upriver some ten years prior. He carried a photograph in his shirt pocket and took it out often to admire. I loved seeing that – how similar my friend and I were no matter the differences that divided us.

I enjoyed the brass band that played every night on the lower deck. The men held these shining horns in hand, blow into them and tap their feet, eager to carry on a happy tune. A brilliant pianist, said to be a prodigy, played with mirth, her hair floating on the high notes. This was music!

Mr. Twain pointed out the tuba and the clarinet, the French horn and the trombone. There were drums and even a trumpet. I couldn't help but whistle along. The music was awe-inspiring, flooding our floating ferryboat and spilling out into the night air with the frogs and crickets and the whirring cicadas. For a moment, I wished Constance could be there to hear it, for I thought this might just be the most beautiful sound under the heavens. I wanted to share it with her, standing beside me in the moonlight. But we never encountered any other mockingbirds on our journey. I was alone on the water with my reflection.

We traveled upriver four days before we put into a little port where Mark Twain and Robert stepped off to have a drink and stretch their legs. I decided to decline, preferring instead the warmth of the morning sun on the deck. Summer was waning. The light was changing, becoming more golden and distant, and there was a new scent of dried leaves in the breeze. Summer would not be with us forever.

I decided to take Mr. Twain's advice and begin rewriting my book. I wanted to capture each memory before it faded. I missed my parents, and Sissy and Earle and Possum. I missed Lolly. I missed our crepe myrtle tree, and its pink blossoms bobbing in the breeze. If I couldn't go home, I could still remember my home, and go there on a page of crisp white paper stained with black ink.

Mark Twain praised my progress. I was making fewer mistakes, he said. And I noticed that his corrections of my grammar and spelling were becoming more infrequent. The hours I spent writing in the early mornings were the happiest moments of my days, just like the brass band filled my lonely heart with contentment in the evenings.

"Writing is a responsibility," said Mr. Twain. "And you're learning the craft very well. I expect you to keep practicing every day. I notice that you use plain, simple language, short words and brief sentences. That is the way to write English – it is the modern way and the best way. Stick to it; don't let fluff and flowers and verbosity creep in. When you catch an adjective, kill it. No, I don't mean utterly, but kill most of them – then the rest will be valuable. They weaken when they are close together. They give strength when they are wide apart. An adjective habit, or a wordy, diffuse, flowery habit, once fastened upon a person, is as hard to get rid of as any other vice."

I nodded. Then I took out the page and spelled out

H-A-P-P-Y

Mr. Twain nodded and lit his cigar. "That's exactly right."

"How far we goin' north, Mista Twain?" asked Robert one afternoon when they had returned from the port town.

"All the way to St. Louis." He seemed lighter since we had struck out on the water. He was freer inside. The river clearly thrilled him. Though he may have looked old by this time in his life, he was every way a young man inside.

Robert looked grave. "Supposing the people up there treat me like … well, like Mista Dixon did?"

"People of his ilk are everywhere, unfortunately. Travel may be the only cure. You see, I find that travel is fatal to prejudice, bigotry, and narrow mindedness. Would that I could stay a few days with you there, but I will need to move on east toward Virginia, where my daughter is waiting to take me north with her to Connecticut."

Robert whistled. "Whew-wee! All the way to St. Louis. I heard all my life bout that city, and it'll be a real honor to see her in person. What do you think, Wynne?"

I shrugged. I had never heard of St. Louis. It seemed a little strange to make such a fuss over a crowd of buildings.

"Perhaps you'd like to come with me, Wynne. You'd like Connecticut," said Mr. Twain. "Besides, I could use the company." He winked at me.

I closed my eyes and dipped my head in respect. Then I shook my head.

"But you can't, is that it?" asked Mark Twain.

I nodded and spread out my wings.

"Well, if you ever change your mind, I'll make sure you have my address so you can write me," said Mr. Twain, his mustache lifting with his smile. "True friends are rare, you know. And as dismayed as I may be to lose your company, I understand you need to finish your quest." Then he added, "But don't fret about it, Wynne. Sometimes what you're looking for has a way of finding you. All you have to remember is always do right, because this will gratify some people and astonish the rest." He thought a moment and added, "Why don't you let me take your book along with me? You can just send the final chapters when you're finished with it. How's that?"

I nodded, my eyes tearing up.

At that moment, a photographer came by dragging his enormous camera and tripod. "You like your picture made, Mister?" he said to Mark Twain.

"Why yes, indeed," said Mark Twain. He invited Robert and I to come stand beside him on the rail of that ferryboat, and the photographer set up and got inside his camera curtain and then there was a big click and a flash of light.

That photograph of us became my most treasured possession. It replaced the one of Mark Twain I had lost in the tornado. These were my friends, my true friends.

The next afternoon was one of the hottest of late summer. The breeze was stingy, and our progress was so slow up the river it felt as if we weren't moving at all. I grew impatient on the deck, watching Mark Twain and Robert play shuffleboard. I decided to walk the perimeter of the ship along the polished rail. The captain's daughter was out, skipping rope near the stern. She waved a beaming hello to me, her pigtails flouncing in the breeze. I thought of Mary-Liz fondly then, and how she had rescued me from the Grey Cat those many moons ago.

Lost in my reverie, the ferryboat jolted in the water for an instant, and it was just long enough for me to lose my footing on the slick, well-oiled rail. I fell backwards, beak over feet, fluttering to right myself. As I looked down, tumbling through the air, I saw my little mishap couldn't have been more poorly timed; I had been perched directly over the churning ferry wheel, the massive sharp blades spinning end over end in the water.

I closed my eyes and prepared for the worst, knowing that once I got under those mighty blades, I would be pushed down to the bottom of the river, and that would be the end of me.

But the death I had expected seemed to take forever. I braced myself for the cold river water to wash over me, but I stayed warm and dry.

I cracked my eyes open and dared to look out.

Why, I was up in the sky! My wings were fully outstretched, and there I was, soaring high up over the riverboat. I turned a few circles and felt the ecstasy of the movement, stretching out my feathers to test their strength. The sky never felt so right to me before.

In a flight of joy I soared upward, high up over the ferryboat, and looked down to see Mark Twain and Robert at the rail, waving up to me. "Look, there! It's Wynne!" called Robert.

"Goodbye, Wynne!" called out Mark Twain, taking off his hat to wave it. "Be sure to write us, now!"

I narrowed my eyes and looked down, and swooped as fast as I could fly down past the rail of the ferryboat. This was my goodbye; my way of showing them how well my wing had healed.

The men cheered and applauded, and I soared up high again and circled in the air, wondering where to set out.

My musings weren't needed for long, however, because I soon saw a familiar shape down among the reeds where a small stream let out into the river. It was a beaver, patting down the last log of a beaver dam with her tail.

"Lolly!" I shouted out.

I swept down out of the sky and landed right on top of the dam with a perfect arch.

"Why, W-w-wynne!" said Lolly, looking up at me in recognition. "I just knew you had to survive that storm. And you look m-m-magnificent! Look at you! Children?" Lolly called out into the bushes, and lo and behold, three young beavers appeared. "This is the special mockingbird I've been telling you all about," said Lolly. "Wynne, meet Savannah, Adelaide, and Frank." Each smiled. Between their legs appeared four more little fuzzy beaver faces. "And my grandchildren," said Lolly. "The eldest is Bernice, and there are the triplets Earnest, Blake, and Francis. Say hello to Wynne, little ones."

I shook each of their paws and complimented Lolly on her fine dam and handsome brood. It was a deep relief and a wonderful joy to find her alive and happy.

"When the creek swept me off and I finally clamored out," said Lolly, "I was so f-f-fortunate as to find my young'uns. We've been together ever since."

I promptly produced the photograph of myself with Robert and Mark Twain. This greatly impressed her grandchildren, who fought to hold it.

"You found your family yet, Wynne?" asked Lolly.

I shook my head.

"My, that's too bad. But you know, little Bernice here, she knows somebody who can help, don't cha?"

The young beaver who went by the name of Bernice nodded and smiled and slapped her tail in delight. "I sure do! Let's go right away. Come on, Wynne!"

We took off through the woods to the edge of a mighty swamp. The trees were all flooded here, and the sky grew a bit darker for the thick brambles. I was overcome with curiosity about who such a young beaver knew that might be able to help me.

"Mama said you've been lookin' for the Skumpletun," said Bernice.

"The Skumpletun!" I had nearly forgotten about our quest to find this mysterious creature. "Do you really know where he is?"

"Sure," said Bernice. "She's right over there, see?"

"She?"

"Oh yes, the Skumpleton is the oldest, wisest grandmother of these woods."

The mist on the ground lifted slightly in the middle of the bog to reveal a stooped old skeleton of a bird, hunched down in her feathers, her beak nearly dragging in the water. At first glance I had to wonder if she dead. But as soon as she heard us, this majestic bird came to life, lifting her long blue neck and spinning to peer at us with round black eyes that I was sure could see straight into my soul.

"What kind of bird *is* that?" I whispered aloud. I had never seen such a large bird, so stoic and regal and frightening. A crest of feathers lifted and fell on the back of her head as she breathed, and her legs hung miles down from her body. She was grey as a winter morning.

"She's a great blue heron," said Bernice matter-of-factly. "I come visit her sometimes so she won't be lonely. All her children have long since flown away. The animals say she's old as stone. Might have lived for twenty winters or more. I'm sure she can help you find your way home. Let's ask."

I felt intimidated approaching this enormous bird, thirty times my size. Why, the top of my head scarcely reached her knees! She looked down at me with a glare that made me shake with nerves.

Finally, she spoke with a voice that rattled and shook. "Good evening."

"Good evening," I croaked.

"Hi, Ol' Skumpletun!" Bernice smiled up at the bird whose bones creaked when she turned her head. "This here's Wynne, and he's lost."

"I see," said the Skumpletun. "Welcome, Wynne. Don't be afraid. I won't hurt you."

"I was born in a place called the Willem Woods," I said, finding my courage. "I hope my family is still there."

The Skumpletun closed her eyes. Then she opened them and nodded. "Yes, I knew those woods once. Five days' flight from here, by the north star. Not so far, even on such small wings." She looked me up and down. "Fly strong in the morning and evening and rest at midday. Keep the sun at your back in the morning, and in your eyes in the evening. By night follow the north star and you will come to the Willem Woods."

My heart leapt in my chest. This was the best possible news! Why, to be only five days of flying from my woods—my family— filled me up with hope inside. I thanked the Skumpletun and gave Bernice a big hug. I wanted to set out right away so as not to lose any time. I would miss Lolly and her family, but now that I knew where they lived, I promised Bernice I would come and visit.

I was turning to go when the Skumpletun spoke again. "Another bird of your size came this way several moons ago. He was asking if I had seen a mockingbird, lost in the woods."

My spine grew cold. What if it was Ricketts and the coons?

"The fox called Rusty brought him here. Yes, just about your size, but a little smaller. Young bird."

"Do you remember the bird's name?" I asked.

"No, 'fraid not. Never caught his name. But he was lookin' for you, mockingbird. I'm afraid I'm not much help."

A funny feeling came into me. "Could it be Possum?" I said.

"No, not a possum, definitely a mockingbird," said the Skumpletun.

"No, I mean my younger brother, Possum. We were bonded in the nest, and I saved him from a mean old crow."

"Brothers," said the Skumpletun, her raspy voice tired with even this effort. "I can see a family resemblance. They returned to the Creekside Parlor. I told him I would inform the lost mockingbird if he ever appeared. And there you are, and so I have told you."

"Then I must go to the parlor and get him," I said. My throat went dry at the thought. Here I was so close to my home in the Willem Woods, but I just had to know if Possum had come looking for me. He might be in danger.

"Don't worry, we'll go with you!" said Bernice, her eyes so sweet and innocent.

"No, Bernice," I said. "The Creekside Parlor is not a place for youngsters. I should go alone."

"Is there bad critters there, like coons?" asked Bernice, her velvet beaver brow furrowed in concern.

"Yes, and then some."

"Then you need a disguise!" she announced.

The Skumpletun laughed hoarsely; amused. Her ancient eyes were full of love. "You best be on your way, both of you. The sun will set and the bog is difficult to navigate in the dark."

I thanked her for her time with a deep bow, and promised to write her into the story that I was planning to mail to Mark Twain when I got home.

Ricketts & Rusty

CH. *11*
BAYOU JAIL BREAK

After a breakfast of the freshest riverbank grubs, I said my goodbyes to Lolly and her family and set out on my own for the Creekside Parlor. I had never intended to step foot in that dreadful place again, but I had to go see if Possum was there.

Bernice had a fine idea with a disguise, I decided. I did not want to be recognized, certainly not by Ricketts or the others. I found a long cattail by the creek and broke off the stalk. It made a convincing mustache and cane.

It was a pleasure to fly again, even if it was along the swampy inlets and bogs. I paused to catch worms in the sand for lunch, then set out following the directions the Skumpletun had given me.

By evening, I could hear music coming through the woods from the Creekside Parlor along with the smell of stinkweed and rotting fish.

My heart began to race, and I shook my feathers. I would need to be brave if I planned to pretend my way inside.

The sun hung low in the west when I saw the parlor on its spindly stilts, suspended over the muddy bog. As I stood there gathering the courage to go inside, the sun disappeared, and all the crickets came out and began their chorus. The stars over my head seemed impossibly close. The porch might have been slightly more crooked than the last time I had seen it. I could hear the wood creak and moan as the wind blew. The instant I set foot on the steps, I a grizzly voice at the door said, "Password."

I cleared my throat. "Piggly Miggly."

"Try again."

"Jambalaya jasper."

"It's Friday. You got one more chance to get it right, stranger."

I rubbed my wing tips together and paced back and forth on the porch trying to think of what in the world I could say that would get me inside. Then I remembered: "Buckeye blues."

The door swung open on rusty hinges and I walked inside, past the gruff raccoon who eyed me suspiciously.

It was the same old parlor, all right. There were tables strewn about with foxes and coons and even a few crows bent over them, sipping fermented moss.

A lively game of poker was going on in the corner, and I recognized Rusty the fox.

I scanned the room for Possum, but didn't see another mockingbird, not even Ricketts.

A perfumed skunk sidled up to me and put her arms around my neck. "How about a dance, stranger?"

Perhaps it would be best to just blend in, I thought, and do what everyone else was doing until I got some answers. I nodded and adjusted my mustache, and followed the skunk out onto the dance floor.

We danced to an old ragtime tune, prancing back and forth along the floor and even drawing a smatter of applause from some of the regulars seated at the tables.

Much to my dismay, the skunk snuggled up next to me and said, "My name's Scarlet, what's yours?"

The color drained out of my cheeks and I cleared my throat. "Uh, it's, uh Billoughby." Where I ever thought up such a ridiculous name I have no idea. It just came out my beak.

"Well, big-boy Billoughby. You're mighty handsome. I was thinkin', how'd you like ta..." and whatever she said next was lost as the horn section broke in and drowned out her words. I gave her a big spin and sent her flying right off the dance floor. This gave me a chance to head over to the bar, where some coons were sipping their drinks. I slid in right between them and nodded. They nodded back.

At that instant, the lights came on the stage and I turned around to see Ricketts stride out in his tails and top hat. He began to sing an upbeat ragtime tune, and then did a few dance steps looking sharp. The whole place broke out in applause. Ricketts finished his number with a bow, then turned to the crowd.

"And now, the moment you've all been waiting for! May I present the lovely... Miss Sapphire Breeze!"

Slowly, an enormous cage was lowered from the ceiling right over the whole crowd. There were cheers and screams and hollers from everyone around. The boys all threw their hats in the air. As the rest of the cage came into view and the spotlight struck it, I could not believe my eyes.

It was Constance! I would have recognized her anywhere. "Constance!" I shouted, but my voice was lost in the crowd's uproar.

The gator at the piano got started on a real sultry number, and Constance—who was dripping in silver sequins, pink feathers, and glittering pearls—began to sing and croon to the hooting audience. She looked so unhappy, trapped in that cage.

"Why, they're holding her captive!" I exclaimed.

"Ain't holdin' nobody nothin'," said a voice on the far end of the bar. "She likes it here. And they like her."

Even in the dark I knew who it was that spoke. It was the handsome suitor Constance had flown away with at the races. Seeing he didn't recognize me, I took a few steps toward him. "She sings like an angel," I said.

"Yup, she does that," he said. "Five nights a week." And he pulled out his wallet and fanned out all his money and smiled before putting it back in his pocket.

"Name's Billoughby," I said.

"Mulligan," said the mockingbird before me. "We ain't seen you round these parts before. You workin' with Ricketts?" he eyed me up and down.

"Uh, sure. I am." I straightened my mustache.

"What part of the woods he got you workin'?" Mulligan eyed me up and down.

"I, em, I work alone. Down by the river. Makin' sure nobody finds the Skumpletun." This was a gamble, and I hoped he believed me.

"Ah sure, that old bird ain't dead yet? Will wonders never cease. So, watcha drinkin'?"

I shrugged.

"Bartender, get this bird a roach fizz."

Roach fizz? I watched as a glass came sliding down the bar in my direction with an enormous roach dunked inside, tiny bubbles rising in the air. I tell you, I wasn't the least bit thirsty anymore.

"And another," said Mulligan.

The bartender sent another roach fizz sliding down the bar and Mulligan caught it before it went by. He dunked his beak and downed all the liquid, then let out a huge belch. He reached in and picked up the roach by an antennae, tossed it in the air, and caught it with his tongue so it slid right down his throat. "Bottoms up, Billoughby."

I eyed my disgusting drink. It was imperative I fit in, no matter what. I had to help Constance get out of there. I was sure they were holding her captive. I closed my eyes and drank the whole thing down in one gulp, roach and all. Then I let out an equally loud belch.

Mulligan clapped me on the back. "You're a good fella, all right."

"Say," I ventured, "you haven't seen any other mockingbirds around, have you?"

At this, Mulligan let out a laugh. "That's funny, bird. That's real funny."

I wondered why he had laughed, but smiled and tried to chuckle along. I called over the bartender and ordered, "Another roach fizz for my friend here." The frothing drink came sliding down the bar. Mulligan nodded, clearly pleased. He polished this one off like before.

Constance was still singing, swinging on the perch in the cage. The crowd had drawn closer in admiration. I approached her cage and attempted to get her attention. "Constance," I said, but she couldn't hear me over the music and the cheering. "Constance, it's me, Wynne."

She looked at me and I peeled the cattail from above my beak for an instant.

Her eyes lit up a moment in recognition, but she looked away and continued with her song.

Just then there was an enormous clatter from the kitchen. A whole mess of plates and pans must have hit the floor, because it stopped the piano player mid-note, and we all turned around as the chef, a burly swamp rat swinging a frying pan, came out chasing a young mockingbird wearing a white apron.

"Ricketts, this no good bird can't lift a finger in the kitchen, because he's got no paws, see?" the rat wiggled his stubby fingers and then lifted the wing of the bird by comparison. "You bring me some real help or I quit!"

The young mockingbird then cowered in the corner, covering his face with his wing.

"Damn mockingbirds!" shouted a raccoon. "Soon we'll be rid of 'em all! Cheers!"

The whole bar broke out in applause.

"What's he mean by that?" I leaned over and asked Scarlet the skunk, who had found her way over to me during the ruckus.

"Ricketts is cleanin' up the woods, making all the mockin'birds work for him in the cellar makin' fermented moss. It never tasted better, I say." Scarlet fluttered her eyelashes at me.

I went over to the young bird in the corner and reached down to help him up. He wouldn't take my wing. "You're no good just like the rest of them," said the bird, and he got up and dusted himself off.

"Possum?" I said. I hadn't seen him since we were in the nest, and this bird was full-fledged. I couldn't be sure, but there was something familiar about his voice.

"Who's askin'?" he said.

I removed my cattail mustache for a moment. "It's me, Wynne."

"Wynne!" he hugged my neck. "It is you! I thought I might never find you. I looked everywhere."

"We can't talk here," I said. "I gotta get you and Constance out of here."

"We should try and help the others down in the cellar," said Possum.

"I heard as much," I whispered.

By then Constance was finishing her act. I noticed Mulligan eyeing me suspiciously. "Quick, how do we get down to the cellar?"

"This way," said Possum.

We stepped out into the hall and Possum opened a door that led downstairs.

It got darker as we reached the bottom. There was no light anywhere. The bottom step creaked.

Possum gave a low whistle, and I could hear the flutter of wings as birds in the darkness moved around. Then he reached under the loose step and pulled out a brass key.

"Listen up," said Possum. "This here's a jail break. We got one chance at it. Once we get the key, split up and make a run for it!"

There was a shuffle of agreement.

Possum slid the key in the lock and threw open the iron door, but just then, Ricketts appeared right behind me.

"Who you talkin' to, stranger?" he said.

I turned around and to face Ricketts in all his wickedness. He ripped off my cattail mustache and grabbed my cane. "I know you," he said. "You and the beaver came here and stole money from me earlier this summer."

"I never stole anything from you," I said. "I just came to get my brother."

"Is this little runt your brother?" Ricketts reached around his back and had Possum by the scruff. He saw my eyes drop and smiled. "Well, then you belong together, don't cha?"

With that he threw us into the cellar, and pocketed the key. Then he disappeared up the stairs, whistling snappy tune, entirely pleased with himself.

"Don't worry, Possum. I'll get us outside, somehow," I said. "We'll fly away from this swamp together."

"It's not that easy, Wynne. Ricketts clipped our flight feathers. None of us can fly."

"None of you can fly?" I held up Possum's wings and noticed the feathers all trimmed down on each side.

The heads of twelve other mockingbirds nodded in unison. Old, young, frail, thirsty. Ricketts had locked them all up together in his vengeance for being exiled from the Willem Woods.

"Well, I hope you can run," I said.

We spent the next hour in silence together, just waiting, listening to every stray note of music, every creak on the stairs.

"What's your plan, Wynne?" asked Possum.

"I'm thinkin' of one," I said. "I'm tryin' to think of one anyways."

Just then we heard the tap of footsteps, and the clinking of an iron chain.

Everybody froze in place. Mockingbirds sheltered beneath each other's wings.

"Wynne?" The voice, even though it was quiet as a whisper of wind, I knew instantly.

"Constance?"

"I stole the keys. Come on, everybody. Ricketts is soon to find out!"

She unlocked the iron door, which creaked open far too loudly, and I waited until every mockingbird in the cellar climbed the stairs and made a dash for the woods out the kitchen door.

Possum called to me. "Wynne, you comin'?"

It was too late. The shuffling woke one of the sleepy raccoons, who rang the alarm, an old post office bell above the porch.

"Jail break!" yelled the raccoon. The swamp rat joined in, "Mockingbirds escaping!" He grabbed a spoon and sounded another alarm by banging his frying pan.

The whole bar stopped what they were doing, and I turned around and went back inside. There was chaos as Ricketts and his coons dashed for the door. "You go around the front and head 'em off!" he said to the coons. "Get the others!"

The gators were on their bellies in no time, cutting through the trees. Why, the foxes were just red streaks in the brush.

Constance clung to my arm. Possum stood beside me. What could we do? We frantically looked for direction.

But there, just under the porch, I could see movement. Black shadows under the parlor shifted and disappeared. I thought we might be some terrible bear's dinner when a familiar face peeked out at me from behind one of the rotten posts and smiled. Lolly! She pressed her tail to her nose so I wouldn't shout. In the dim light I could make out her whole family under the parlor, holding on to the stilts with their teeth poised and ready.

There was a great groan in the house.

My eyes went wide. "Ricketts, you all better come off there. The whole parlor is about to be in the mud."

Ricketts laughed at me. "You think I'll fall for an old trick like that?"

"No, I mean it," I said.

Lolly signaled, raising her tail, pinning her ears back. Each of the beavers gnawed their final bites in the pylons beneath the parlor. And that was it. They all dashed out from under the porch to safety and waved at me.

I stood up and brushed the mud off. "Okay," I said to Ricketts. "But don't say I didn't warn you."

With that, I gave the nearest rail on the porch a little shove, and darn if the whole building didn't just collapse right there! The stilts all snapped, and the parlor dropped over on its side with a huge *crash!* and began to sink into the mud.

"Well done, Lolly!" I cheered.

"You better believe it, Wynne," said Lolly.

"You're friends with a beaver?" said Possum.

"One of the greatest beavers that ever lived," I said. "That's my friend Lolly!"

Possum bowed in appreciation.

"Wynne, we need to get out of here," Constance said, pointing with her wingtip at the parlor which was sinking fast. Half the structure was already buried in the mud. Ricketts was holding on to that post, trying with all his might to keep his beloved parlor from sinking any deeper.

Mulligan stepped out of the swamp and strode up to where we were standing. "Constance, you're comin' with me," he said. "You're mine. I love you."

A bolt of fear shot through me. He could tear me to shreds in an instant.

The parlor was nearly out of sight in the mud.

"Mulligan!" cried Ricketts. "Forget her! Save the parlor!"

Mulligan turned his head and saw the parlor sinking, looked back to Constance.

"Constance doesn't belong to anybody," I said. "She's her own bird."

"You don't love me," added Constance. "You really love that old parlor. And look what's gonna happen if you don't do something."

The house moaned, and tilted. Ricketts fought with all his might to keep it from sinking into the bog.

Mulligan pressed his breast against my beak, lifted his wings like he was about to fight me. Then he miraculously backed away. "This ain't the end of it," he said as he joined his pal Ricketts, holding up the other side of the sinking parlor.

Soon both Ricketts and Mulligan were covered in mud and vanishing fast.

"Let's go home, Wynne." Constance pecked me on the cheek.

"Woohoo!" cheered Possum. "Let's go home!"

Well if I didn't just lose my feet and twirled a circle in the air right there—it was the happiest moment of my life.

From behind the trees in the swamp the other mockingbirds cheered and ran ahead.

Meanwhile, Ricketts and Mulligan realized they needed some help under the parlor. Ricketts gave a loud whistle, and all the coons and foxes came streaming back out of the woods and saw what was happening. They quickly stood around the parlor, bracing to pry it up out of the mud, but it was no use. The house sank until the entire bottom floor was lost.

"Now's our chance," I said. "Let's get out of here."

Constance and Possum agreed.

There was an enormous crash, and the Creekside Parlor disappeared down into the mud until there was only the brick chimney left, Mulligan and Ricketts clinging to it in a failed effort to pry it up.

As we dashed through the woods, I could hear Ricketts and Mulligan sobbing, throwing mud at each other with loud *splats!* Those two wouldn't be troubling anybody for a long while, I felt certain.

There was a flash of red, quick like firelight, and a voice whispered, "Come with me."

It was Rusty.

"Wynne, a fox!" cried Constance.

"It's all right," I reassured her. "Rusty helped my brother find the Skumpleton."

Rusty nodded, his eyes shining in the darkness. "We foxes are known for being sly, but not all of us are unkind. Follow me."

Rusty led us through the trees, and I prayed he would be true to his word and not get hungry along the way.

Down by the creek, Rusty disappeared in the thin starlight, and then we saw the other mocking-birds, shivering in the dark. "We can't fly!" one of them said. "How will we get across?"

"The coons and gators will come back for us!" yelled another.

We were trapped at the water's edge.

I thought, and walked, and thought some more, but couldn't imagine an escape.

But then, through the middle of all the birds, Lolly appeared. Behind her were her children and grandchildren. And behind *them* were all their extended family of aunts and uncles and cousins. Why, there must have been at least thirty beavers in all! They formed a chain – nose to tail – and slipped into the creek.

"Beavers!" cried the mockingbirds, each aware of the stigma of associating with what they'd been raised to believe was river rodent slime. "Never."

"Lolly is a dear friend, and beavers deserve our respect," I said. "She's helped all of us escape. We owe them all our thanks!"

The mockingbirds nodded, understanding for the first time the wrong of a century of misplaced prejudice, seeing that our destinies were intertwined.

"All aboard!" said Lolly, and the beavers straightened out their tails so the mockingbirds could walk right up onto their backs from the bank. Possum went with Lolly, but Constance hung back on the shore beside me.

"You better go too, before the coons come back," I said.

But Constance shook her head. "I'm not going anywhere without you." Then she stretched out her wings. "They didn't clip my feathers, Wynne. They had me in that awful cage, so I guess they didn't think of it." She smiled at me.

"Let's go home," I said.

I took off into the sky with Constance wingtip to wingtip. Below us the beavers and their happy mockingbird passengers floated peacefully over the smooth water.

I flew a wide circle over the woods and looked down to see just a few strips of wood where the parlor had been. Ricketts had his head burrowed in his wings, sobbing, Mulligan beside him wiping his tears. The other animals paced the bog, dismayed.

"Looks like you got enough wood there to open yourself up a lemonade stand!" I yelled.

Ricketts didn't even look up. He was ruined.

We soared out over the creek and watched the procession of beavers and mockingbirds floating along in the moonlight. Possum whistled, "I always knew I'd find you, Wynne! I knew no Grey Cat could ever get the best of you!"

I smiled.

We were going home.

CH. *12*

THE WILLEM WOODS

Tuesday.

Mark Twain had been right, and my spelling had improved. I'd been searching for so long for the way home, but sometimes what you're lookin' for has a way of finding you. I called out to Constance from the branch below our new nest. "You hungry for supper, Sweetheart?"

She peeked over the carefully arranged twigs and smiled. "Sure am!"

I flew down to the MacMaster's fence and gave a whistle into the cool evening. The last day of summer was behind us now, and autumn cooled the breeze. I hopped down to the meadow and went searching for crickets that were just coming out in the grass. Once I had my beak full, I swept up into the sky and flew back to our crepe myrtle tree.

Constance smiled at me, her face so warm and rosy I almost forgot the supper in my beak. "Look, Wynne," she said, and she lifted her wing to reveal three little mockingbirds, their open beaks turned to me.

"The eggs hatched!" I said, letting the crickets fall out of my mouth. They didn't escape Constance, who gulped them down in one swift peck.

These were my children looking up at me, their beaks turned upwards in hungry smiles. "Papa!" they shouted. "Papa!" I fell backwards on my tail in the nest and they all jumped on me, covering me with kisses. There were two boys and a girl. "Have you thought of what to call them, yet?" I asked.

Constance smiled. "I thought we'd call the girl Lolly. And the boys Rusty and Robert."

"Awe, shucks," I said. "I'll have to send a letter and let everyone know the good news."

But good news has a way of traveling on its own, and soon enough, all across the Willem Woods the birds were singing the joy of my new family.

Sissy was the first to arrive with gifts, followed by Earle and his wife Ella and their two sons, James and Happy. My parents arrived next, beaming at becoming grandparents for the second time. Possum came next with his new lady, Wilma. And our nest sure was crowed as everyone squawked with enthusiasm at our new arrivals.

My father, Tennessee, pulled me aside and put his wing around my back. "I sure am proud of you, Wynne. I hope you always know it."

"Thanks, Pops," I said, brimming my pride.

"And I got somethin' for ya," he said. He pulled out a letter from under his wing and laid it down in front of me. "Came in the post today."

"Connecticut!" I declared, seeing the postmark. I ripped it open with my beak and unfolded the letter with my feet. It was from Mark Twain.

> Dear Wynne,
>
> I was pleased to receive the completed manuscript of your story *Mockingbird Summer*, and I want you to know I passed it along to my editor, who was equally delighted. She has promised to publish it, and we hope you will be able to attend a party I am hosting for you and your family in celebration. Congratulations on your homecoming, Wynne. You are one special bird.
>
> Your friend,
> Mark Twain

"It came with this parcel," said Honey-Pop, who pushed a large brown package wrapped in twine over to me.

This was almost too much good news to bear. I felt my eyes starting to tear up. Everyone had stopped to watch.

"Go on, open it, Wynne," said Constance.

"Open it, Papa!" echoed the little ones.

"All right," I said. I tugged at the string with my beak till it came loose. I tore open the paper with my feet, and there inside was the most beautiful blue shiny rectangle I'd ever seen.

"Oh, Wynne! It's your book!" said Constance.

My mother beamed.

It was the galley, the very first book off the presses. It was heavy as a brick, and nearly a hundred pages in all. There on the front was the title and right above it, my name above a pretty painting of the Willem Woods, our crepe myrtle tree, and a mockingbird on a fence, his tail lifted in song.

My father passed it to my mother, who adjusted her glasses and read the dedication. Her eyes filled with tears. "We love you, too, Wynne," she said, and she gave me a hug.

It was good to be home.

The reception of my book was excellent among all the birds and critters of the Willem Woods. We threw an imaginative costume party, music to boot, and brought new friends together to celebrate our love of adventure, and appreciation for one another. I blush to think it was for me.

The Grey Cat had long since disappeared, and the coming of autumn meant that Mary-Liz took up walking through the woods to get to school. I would fly down to the MacMaster's fence, wave to her and serenade her with a round of "Golden Slippers" nearly every morning.

Life wasn't perfect, but I tell you, it was darn close. I was now a published author, which meant I had responsibilities. I decided to open a school of my own and teach all the young birds in the Willem Woods to spell and write and count. My school was very popular, and soon we had to move it to the top of the old barn so there was enough room for the youngsters' parents to join as well, since everyone valued an education.

I wrote Mark Twain a letter, thanking him and promising we'd visit him for the party. And I hung the photograph of Twain, myself, and Robert over our nest. A letter had come the week before from Robert saying he had been admitted to the university, and he was well on his way to becoming a lawyer. There was a photograph enclosed of him and his father, reunited at last.

Every so often I would take a little trip east and visit Lolly and her family on the river. They were all getting along fine. I promised my own children that when they were old enough to fly I would take them with me to visit the beavers they were named after.

Time and again, we read my book. Everyone wanted to hear the story of the tornado, how I signed my wing, and of Ricketts and the Creekside Parlor, and of Lolly and her family, again and again. Constance would read, and I would act out the parts on a little stage we built on a lower branch with the fireflies hanging over me to light up the darkness.

One night at bedtime, my children gathered around me. Lolly, my eldest, asked, "Papa? Will we have adventures like yours?"

Robert, the youngest, piped up. "You think we'll ever see the Grey Cat?"

"Or the Mississippi River?" asked Rusty.

I sat back and put my wing over Constance. "Children, life is long, and you have plenty of time to live it. Enjoy your nest and your family, and before you know it, you'll be grown and having adventures of your own."

Constance smiled at me and we snuggled into our nest beside our fledglings, listening to the thrum of the crickets and cicadas as we drifted off to sleep.

THE END

ACKNOWLEDGEMENTS

My grandmother, Sissy, was a lifelong reader. She held a monthly book club in Wynne, Arkansas until she was nearly ninety years old. My grandfather, Daddyman, enjoyed books, too, and although he mostly read westerns he delighted in my stories. My grandparents were always heading to the library with armfuls of books they intended to read or return. I'm so deeply thankful to them both for instilling in me a lineage and love of reading.

I'm grateful to my mother, Shannon, for being an enthusiastic reader of mine, realizing I'm forever spoiled at thinking I must be a somewhat decent writer, if she's entertained. I'm thankful to my stepfather, Scotty, who has encouraged and supported my writing from the moment he entered my life. I have rare parents who know how to love, and I recommend their book, *The Love You Deserve*.

Thank you, Gayle Gladstone, who made it possible for you to read this novel, and to the amazing Bill Gladstone, my literary agent and partner in believing.

Thank you to my son, Atticus. I started writing this book when he was in utero, and he was a reader of other drafts (at age 6), making important requests about what happens to the characters, and how he wanted it to end.

Thank you to Garry Shandling, and Tom Robbins, my mentors, who taught me that the work is all that matters, that you love it, and that you dedicate your whole heart to it.

Thank you to my reader, to you, for being part of Wynne's journey. Without you, as your author I wouldn't be here at all, so that makes you very important, indeed.

Finally, thank you to Mark Twain, who always seemed to find a way to laugh at whatever circumstances arose. I hope he inspires you to do the same.

ABOUT THE AUTHOR

K aia Alexander is an award-winning novelist, mom, filmmaker, historian and surfer residing in her beloved coastal town of Encinitas, California.

About the Illustrator

Elaina Scott is an American Animator who has worked in video games, film and television as well as a web series by Chuck Jones. She enjoys writing and drawing as well as animating. She graduated from the Character Animation Department at California Institute of the Arts in 2002.

Made in the USA
Columbia, SC
23 October 2020